D0525664

The Milliner and
the Phrenologist

KAY SYRAD

Cinnamon Press
Independent Innovative International

Published by Cinnamon Press
Meirion House,
Glan yr afon,
Tanygrisiau,
Blaenau Ffestiniog,
Gwynedd, LL41 3SU
www.cinnamonpress.com

The right of Kay Syrad to be identified as the author of this work has been asserted by her in accordance with the Copyright, Designs and Patent Act, 1988. © Kay Syrad 2009.
ISBN 978-1-905614-71-4
British Library Cataloguing in Publication Data. A CIP record for this book can be obtained from the British Library

All the characters in this book are fictitious and any resemblance to actual persons, living or dead, is purely coincidental.

Designed and typeset in Garamond by Cinnamon Press. Cover design by Mike Fortune-Wood from original artwork 'Silk Lace Texture' by Eve Le Tova & 'Callipers' by Stillfx' © agency: dreamstime.com. Printed and bound in Great Britain by MPG Book Group, Bodmin & King's Lynn.

Cinnamon Press is represented in the UK by Inpress Ltd www.inpressbooks.co.uk and in Wales by the Welsh Books Council www.cllc.org.uk.

For Chris Drury,
my parents Gill and John Syrad,
and my daughters, Amy and Mari

I

1851

Dr. John Motton opens the door to welcome his next client. Ah, but she is really most handsome, and voluptuous, and tall; she moves most gracefully across the Room. She descends carefully on to the designated chair. She sits on the edge of the chair in her hooped skirts; she sits a little forward, very demure. Dr. Motton eases behind his desk, gesturing towards his callipers and the porcelain head.

'Do you wish yourself to be delineated, my dear, or perhaps you have come about a relative?'

She is perhaps twenty-six or twenty-eight, very fine proportions; indeed, he thinks, she should be exhibited at the Great Exhibition, so fine a woman as this.

'No, Sir—I merely wish to understand a little of myself.'

'How very sensible, my dear. Well then, let me first of all take a few particulars.'

He asks her name, her address and, coughing slightly, her age. Each piece of information Mrs. Isabella Raleigh gives without hesitation, her voice velvet smooth.

'Now, tell me a little about your life, my dear, and about your parentage,' he encourages.

She is, she purrs, the daughter of a Surrey gentleman, now deceased; her mother died in the childbirth of her younger brother. She married young, the gentleman Robertson Raleigh, who was killed, most tragically, two years previously in a hunting accident. She now lives, she explains, under the excellent care and affection of her brother, who is soon to be ordained into the Anglican

Church. A widow: he only now notices her black collar and cuffs, the jet brocade on her dark green coat.

'Now, my dear, you see these callipers, they are of the finest manufacture. See this polished brass hinge, for example, and the beauty of this curve, arced to the specifications of the best Phrenologists in Edinburgh. So, if you would keep very, very still.'

He places the callipers over Isabella's handsome head; the crow-black curls are lush between the glistening brass arcs. Dr. Motton peers closely at the callipers and turns a little screw. He breathes in; jasmine, he thinks. He eases the callipers off, takes up his satin and leather tape from its lacquered box and measures the distance he has just created. He writes numbers in his book, looks at his chart, and returns to this—beautiful—woman perched on the edge of her chair. He moves the callipers round to the back of her head, measuring the distance between her crown and her elegant jaw: this side, and the other side. As he does this, Dr. Motton must touch her hair, her scalp, and her neck. He must touch her cerebellum, and once he grazes her ear. Her perfume is a little too powerful for his taste, but he can endure it.

Now, as he quickly writes, he feels the frisson of discovery; he feels pride, like that of a father, as if he himself has created this fine specimen. And he knows at once: both *Amativeness* and *Conjugality* are strong, together with good *Veneration* and excellent *Benevolence*. He notes that all her *Perceptive* organs are satisfactory, and that *Imitation* is large; he knows, indeed, that all she suffers from is—*Perfection*.

'The measuring is complete, my dear.'

Ah, she will be a fine and dutiful wife with this combination, and he begins to think of friends of his who are in need of a fine wife. He begins to think of the prestige of introducing the young woman. But surely he needs to measure her again. He needs to ensure he is absolutely correct if he is to recommend the pretty widow to his gentleman friends.

'If you would kindly return in two days' time, at three o'clock, I shall repeat the measurements—good science requires repetition, Madam—and shortly after that, I shall be in a position to present you with your chart. Payment may be deferred until that time, thank you.'

Isabella leaves, and Dr. John Motton slips out after her. He follows her to Holland Park Rise where he watches her go up some steps and disappear behind a blue door with elaborate stained glass in its windows. Then he hurries home. He has another client in forty minutes and he has failed to mention to his wife that he was stepping out for a little air. He hurries home thinking about the preparation of his chart for Mrs. Isabella Raleigh. She is really a model woman: she has everything a man could desire, and everything necessary to be a good wife and citizen.

Later, in the evening, he swivels on his leather chair and lights up a pipe of tobacco. He finishes writing the provisional chart. It is as he thought: Mrs. Isabella Raleigh, widow, is indeed a perfect specimen. She is modest and conjugal and has good artistic sense for the making of a beautiful home. She is honest and kind, of vital temperament, good intelligence—*Language* in particular. Moreover, she is beautiful and vigorous, sound of mind and judgement and she has another appointment here with him, Dr. John Motton, on Wednesday afternoon. Now his wife Belinda comes in, fussing with the flowers in the vase on the window ledge.

'Leave those!' he cries.

Belinda is startled. 'Yes, dear.' And she backs out of the Room like a servant.

He feels remorse but he does not go to comfort her. The flowers are yellow roses, rather over-blown, he admits, but he wants them there when Mrs. Raleigh arrives. They are his favourite flowers.

It is Wednesday. She arrives. She wears a black coat with a dark green collar now, and carries a matching umbrella. Her lips are red, her cheeks are pink with the cool air. Her black eyes shine out.

'Ma'am.'

Motton finds himself bowing. She is seated opposite him once more, very calm, he observes; seemingly neither apprehensive nor especially curious. He has written the provisional analysis in his very best script (indeed, he tore up the first chart on account of one small mistake).

'Let me explain, Mrs. Raleigh.' He draws up a chair next to the woman. He explains the chart. She looks gratified, she smiles; she smiles at him. He is in her orbit, within the strong fragrance of her. He takes up her hand. He kisses her hand.

Dr. Motton can hear his wife in the hallway. He predicts that in approximately fifteen seconds she will call out in her thin, shrill voice. She calls out,

'John, dear, our son Johnny says he won't have the daguerreotype made.'

'Won't?'

Belinda steps into the Room. 'He insists it will not be a good likeness.'

Dr. Motton closes the door behind his wife, who remains diminutive despite her ballooning skirts. 'Then he is exceedingly vain, my dear—and *Combative*, and *Destructive* in the extreme.'

'Yes, dear.'

'And *Secretive*. Send Mary to fetch him. Let him show us the exact degree of his perverted *Combativeness*.'

Belinda Motton's features are pointed and small as she calls for Mary.

Mary finds him at once, as she always does. Today the younger John Motton returns to the house flushed with a new knowledge.

'Come in, young Sir.' The father beckons the son into his Room. 'Sit down there.'

The father is aroused, he begins to pace, to strut, his clean movements become irregular.

'You are twenty years of age. I can no longer beat you. But I would very much like to beat you—for your pride, young man, for your *Secretiveness.*'

John gazes beyond his father as if towards the bookcases. He is mesmerized by what he has just experienced at the top of Silver Street. A finely-dressed woman of perhaps twenty-five or thirty had moistened her lips with her tongue as he stepped aside to let her pass at the narrow bend, and then she had slipped a printed card into his hand. It was in his pocket now. It could fall from his pocket at any moment. His father is unpredictable, he could lunge at his son, wield a pair of callipers. He is strutting; he watches his father strutting. He knows his father will stop soon, that he will stand stock-still to begin the disassembly of his son's character. That he will remark upon, with white knuckles, the entirely unacceptable combination of his son's propensities. The son moves his thoughts back to the printed card: Mrs. Raleigh of Holland Park Mansions. Mrs. Raleigh, who moistened her lips with her tongue as she pressed a printed card into a young man's hand. Then he feels it. It begins as heat across the back of his neck; and another wave of heat. He crouches, clasping his hands together behind his head. His mother is shrieking. She leans over him now, grasps his wrist, tries to pull him out of the Room.

*

Dr. John Motton studies Mrs. Raleigh's Phrenological Chart, the one he copied out from the original. He keeps it in the small top left-hand drawer of his desk and he looks at it every morning before he begins his day's work. Today he reads it and closes his eyes, as he does every morning, to imagine the woman, the woman whose beauty is manifest in her moral character just as it is in her face.

On the opposite wall is the new daguerreotype of his son. Regrettably, the silhouette seems to accentuate those very organs of his son's head that should rather be discreet. He will have an oil portrait commissioned next year, for his son's birthday; perhaps it will be kinder to the young man.

Mary comes in with his coffee and toast. Everything is exactly as he likes: the toast cut into triangles and slotted into a silver rack; butter and marmalade on plates painted over with tiny blue pagodas, and all laid out carefully on a starched white tray cloth. Mary is a good girl, new; he made her delineation only two months ago, before he and Belinda could agree to take her on. Yes, a good girl, modest, occasionally a little bit excitable. Of course, he could see straight away at the first interview that the girl would be neat and orderly in her work: the centre of her forehead was full, her eyes were not sunken at all but very open and fresh, and her eyebrows, moreover, were full at the corners.

Dr. Motton spreads a little marmalade on his toast. He takes a sip of his coffee. The sun shines in through the windows: light falls on his breakfast and on his copy of George Combe's *Constitution of Man*. In fact, the sunlight is glinting on the curves of the porcelain head; ah, now it is falling directly, and charmingly, on *Benevolence*. It is nine o'clock. He looks again at Isabella's Chart, and places it back in the drawer. In half an hour his first client of the day will be arriving. He has time to call his son down for a fifteen-minute discussion on the Organ of *Wonder*.

Johnny appears before him at the desk, and for a moment Dr. John Motton ceases to breathe. His son is wearing one of his own, one of his own very best, yellow silk cravats. The pale primrose Indian silk: the Paterson. Dr. John Motton pushes away his tray of breakfast.

'Mother insisted...' starts Johnny. 'I'm giving my first Lecture at the Club this afternoon—you remember.'

It is surely greasy, his son's neck, wrapped illegitimately in the best pale silk.

'*Wonder,*' the father hisses. 'Let us discuss the Organ of *Wonder.* Please, close your eyes and find it on the model.'

The son closes his eyes and steps forward. He stumbles as he feels toward the phrenological head. It falls to the floor. Miraculously it is not broken, its fall softened by the Persian rug. The head lies on its side, *Wonder* to the fore.

'There, look at that!' says the young man jocularly. '*Wonder*—look at the light shining on it now.'

The two men bend down over the head. Dr. John Motton is experiencing a constriction in his chest. The head is a little dusty from the rug; the young Motton pulls out his handkerchief ready to polish. From his pocket there also falls a little visiting card and it lies there between the two men, illuminated by the morning sun.

Mrs. Isabella Raleigh,
6b Holland Park Mansions W.

The words are printed in red ink. There is a decorative black swirl under the address. The father looks at the son. The son looks at the card. The father looks at the card. There is a strange silence in Dr. John Motton's head, a void. The two men are crouched over the phrenological head and the visiting card and the silence continues. Then the clock is ticking, and the young man is saying, very casually, that the woman pressed the card into his hand the other day—just outside in the street—he presumed she was a prostitute —not that he would ever visit a prostitute, of course—and he'd stuffed it into his pocket and forgotten about it. He says all this with a sort of caddish, bullish pride.

The father stands up. 'You're lying, boy,' he says, very low. The son stands up too. The father now repeats the words at a much greater volume. 'You're lying. Where did you get this card? What do you mean, she "pressed it into your hand in the street"? Who did? When?'

The young man steps backwards.

'It's nothing, Sir, just one of those tarts—you know, high class tarts—at the top of Silver Street…'

The father is pushing the son out of the Consulting Room, the young man is resisting, uncomprehending; he pushes back. The two are joined, the father is trying to get the boy out of the house, the front door is being pulled open, Mary is at the back of the hallway, Belinda is at the door of the drawing room. The older man pushes his son on to the steps, the two stumble down, the father pushing the son hard against the railings. They are on the pavement, they are one, shirt-tails and jackets, the yellow cravat is off, lying on the pavement. The two men are in the road.

Someone is screaming. Mary is there, someone is holding Mother back at the top of the steps.

The driver of a hansom is doubled over, being sick. Dr. John Motton's head is covered with his son's jacket.

II

1865

Alice Heapy sat at her bare window. Whatever was outside was obscured by the smoke from the chimneys of the laundry. But what was inside pleased her immensely: there was no wallpaper to distract her (no leaves, no flowers, no lemons cascading over everything), no fringes plunging down over the furniture, and no drab drapes. No, here it was plain, just her worktable, scrubbed and strong, and in orderly rows against the white wall, her blocks and threads and netting, her linens and silks, and, in the corner, a pyramid of hatboxes, each painstakingly acquired.

Alice was alone here, Mother was dead, brother Edward was in thrall to his new pink wife, and now that she had left Madame's, she would not be disturbed by apprentice milliners squawking and crying in the night. No. Here, she could dress and undress leisurely. She could sing or laugh. She could work all night if she must, waiting for the sun to rise, and then lie down flat on the bed with only the light covering her. In fact, she often worked all night, her fingers and stitches flickering in the candle flame, her nose pointed with the cold and her eyes stinging. When she felt overcome by sleep she marched across her room, hither, thither, widening her eyes, clapping her hands, and wrapping herself tight round with Mother's big, faded tartan shawl.

She didn't have a shop yet, and she couldn't call herself Madame, but she already had three ladies who had chosen her, Alice, from all the milliners in London: the voluminous Mrs. Zaphinov, the mysterious Miss Thirsk—and now a Mrs. Belinda Motton, of Church Street, Kensington. At first it was just Mrs. Zaphinov, before Alice went to work at Madame's, Mrs. Zaphinov, with her sugary peach skin, just before Mother had died, surging into Alice's house and demanding she urgently finish the bonnet for her cousin's wedding. There they'd been, Alice and young Edward, trying to keep Mother dry or damp or cool or warm, and Edward trying to convince Mother that Father was dead, that he had been dead ten years.

'No, Edward, I can hear him,' Mother had insisted. 'He's in the front parlour. He's calling me—*Lily! Lily!*'

She could no longer touch the roof of her mouth with her tongue; she had to breathe the words from her throat. Again Edward tried to explain but Mother admonished him, '*Ssshhh! Listen!*' and sat bolt upright, with the three of them waiting there in the silence, with Mother's beef tea cold on her tray. She, with her bulbous eyes, their heavy lids dropping down until barely a slit of white showed, and her terrible mouth—and the two, Alice and Edward, waiting, and watching her and weeping.

Edward repeating quietly, 'He's dead, Mother. Please don't say he's there in the front parlour.'

And Alice thinking of Father bent over the kitchen table taking the barometer apart, the cogs oily between his thick fingers. Then Mother's breathing becoming almost indiscernible so that they began to rock her and clasp at her hands and arms until she tipped forward, knocking her tea over and they could only watch as the dark liquid spread into the green satin bedspread.

Alice had been trying to prop Mother up when the doorbell rang, long and insistent, and it was Mrs. Zaphinov arriving. Edward opened the door, but seeing Alice emerge from Mother's room at the end of the hallway, Mrs. Zaphinov had swept past him, announcing that she really should not have had to make this visit herself, but her maid had injured her leg and could not walk.

'Of course I don't believe it for a *minute*,' she'd boomed, 'but you see, Miss Heapy, I *must* have my new hat by the morning for I'm going to stay with my cousin for a week before the wedding and I must of course take the hat with me.'

Alice could smell the woman's perfume. Mrs. Zaphinov did not begin and end in a definite way: she was blouse, jasmine, jonquil.

'Could you, Miss Heapy? Could you finish my hat by the morning? Answer me, my dear!'

'The trouble is, ma'am...'

Mrs. Zaphinov bore down on Alice, her huge bosom heaving. 'Then I shall send a boy to collect it at half past nine.'

By half past nine I could be dead, thought Alice, Mother could be dead, and Mrs. Zaphinov could be dead, with goose feathers over her eyes.

'Miss Heapy, what *is* the matter?'

Edward had stepped forward then, his young heart beating out for justice, explaining to Mrs. Zaphinov that Mother was most unwell, that Alice could not be expected to finish the hat that night—perhaps by the end of the week. Mrs. Zaphinov had looked at Edward and Alice as if a wasp was buzzing behind her eyes, and she left the house noisily, casting furious commiserations through her peach silk glove. '*Half past nine!*'

Alice wept a little now, recalling how she had tried to finish the bonnet whilst Edward sat with Mother all night, Mrs. Zaphinov's boy arriving exactly at half past nine, and waiting, tapping his fingers and his foot and sighing and yawning until half past ten, when Alice handed over the bonnet in a big peach-coloured box. Mother died the next day, and it wasn't long after that when Alice went into the dormitory at Madame D'Acier's establishment and Edward got a job at the hat blockers, sleeping in the back parlour at Joseph's. Mother, Mother, Mother!

The window panes were almost dark now. Alice unwrapped a piece of bread from her cupboard. Tomorrow she would buy candles for her night-work; tonight she would undress leisurely and lie in bed with her eyes closed, let herself think of Joseph kissing her, the way he'd pressed her to him, pulled her hair to bring her face towards his, but she fell asleep quickly, and dreamt that she was caught in a mighty wind in Kensington Gardens, trying to catch the autumn leaves in her skirts. Among the scarlet leaves she found a star-shaped pincushion that she'd lost the year before, and then she noticed that all the leaves were folded and pinned into the shape of little boats. But when she tried to sail the boats on the pond, the pins pricked her fingers until they bled. She started to wash away the blood and then Edward was there, scooping up the water and watching it drop slowly through his fingers. *Edward! Edward!*

There was a rapping at the door. It was Mrs. Peake, Alice's landlady. '*Miss Heapy!* Com*mo*tion!' she hissed. 'Quieten down, Miss, you're disturbing my other residents!'

Mrs. Peake: her hearing was profound; she never slept, merely listened, and heard. Alice sat up to look out at the sky. Pins of rain were striking the windowpane and an image of Edward's wedding last year came into Alice's mind. It had been pouring with rain on that day too. Poor Edward—if only he didn't need to save people. He had rescued Cassandra when she was starving and about to offer herself to the Kensington Cavalry, but from the minute she was saved she grew like a cuckoo in a starling's nest, much bigger and greedier than Edward or anyone could ever have imagined, as if her main business in the world was to eat starlings' eggs. And now Edward—thin

16

and bearded, his shoulders hunched and his spine slightly curved at the top, and his little starlings' legs—was hopelessly trying to support the giant cuckoo.

The rain pressed in. Alice brought her blanket up around her ears. Marriage: Miss Heapy, un-married; Miss Thirsk, un-married; Mrs. Zaphinov: widowed; Mrs. Peake, widowed. Her own dead mother, widowed. Alice was twenty-five and unmarried. It could have been Joseph. After all, he was a tailor, a Utopian Socialist—Father would have been pleased—he was the older brother of Edward's childhood friend, and he wore a perfectly-fitting black serge suit. During the first weeks of her and Edward's mourning he'd brought them food parcels from his mother and a little sampler she had made. Here it was, framed, by the bed. In fact, that day Joseph brought the sampler, they had started talking about the stitching in it, and then about measuring, and proportion. Joseph had said he knew how to balance a man out; knew which fabrics and styles and colours rendered a short man taller and a tall man shorter. Alice had begun to notice his wide open face with its broad nose and high cheek bones, his liquid eyes. He'd insisted that he knew what fabric would best suit a particular man, that if he could he would make beautiful expensive suits for the poorest men in the land and put the richest men in rags for a day, a week or a year—to see how minds were changed. He would do it, he'd cried, snatching up Alice's hand, he would make suits for poor men, from left-over or discarded fabric. He would tell the rich man that the fabric was a little more expensive than it actually was, that the tailors would need a little more fabric than they needed, and then with a big, rich man's wastefulness he would make a suit for a small poor man. And when Edward went out to get some coal Joseph brought Alice's hand up to his mouth and drew her towards him. 'Joseph—I'm in mourning,' she'd started, but he'd kissed her hands, saying, 'Yes, and you need comfort at this time, dear Alice, comfort.'

The next day Alice had waited for Joseph in the park. A child was playing in the autumn leaves, clutching them up to her chest and letting them fall and her nurse-maid was gossiping to another, and Joseph, wearing a black tailcoat and white collar strode towards her, opened his mouth and placed it over hers, rather too wide, and whilst the nursemaids gossiped and the child clutched at the crackling leaves, they kissed in this wet, open-mouthed way, then drawing back, as if suspicious of themselves, and laughing into their hands.

Joseph visited Alice almost every evening for three weeks, always arriving an hour before Edward, and Alice let her heart beat hard after its months of numb silence, until Edward came home early one day from the hat blockers — he'd been laid off—and seeing their red faces, sat down at the table and, with his eyes lowered, asked Joseph to leave the house. Alice protested, expecting Joseph to demand an explanation, even to announce their engagement, but without even a glance at Alice, he slipped out of the room, closing the door silently behind him. And Edward, blushing and avoiding Alice's eyes, whispered that Joseph would shortly be marrying another girl—she worked with him at the hat blockers—she was expecting a baby and Joseph had said he would marry her; the banns were being read next week.

It was a little boy, the baby, probably born wearing a black serge suit.

That was more than a year ago and Edward had been taken back at the hat blockers and Alice had spent twelve months at Madame D'Acier's. Now she thought that being married would make her too visible, that marriage rendered a woman both private and public property at once; in the private ownership of another, and yet in a public cage. But she also knew that with each succeeding year, her spinsterhood would render her visible too, she would be visibly *un*married. Thus she needed a veil for spinsterhood, a double veil, in fact, because a part of her had been awakened by Joseph, such that she needed a veil to conceal herself from herself.

And then there was Miss Thirsk, who only received visitors during the evening, and who, on that first occasion, had taken Alice's hand into her own and led her silently into the parlour. She was wearing a Japanese satin gown printed over with mauve and blue lilies, and the parlour was decorated with ink-blue ginger jars and china plates. She had asked Alice to sit down by the fire and then folded down opposite her with her legs to one side, and her head to the other. Her hair fell loosely over one shoulder, exposing her long graceful neck. She had a slight malformation of the top lip, it was swollen and a small scar drew the lip up on the right side. Alice beheld, for the first time, a woman's masculine beauty.

Miss Thirsk spoke very little but her eyes told Alice what she needed to know. They were large, dark brown, and the whites were trimmed with red. Her eyes said that she wanted a sorrowful bonnet that would bring a man towards her, the sort of man who liked a woman to have a sadness of which she never spoke. But Alice already had in mind a design that would match Miss Thirsk's grace, a bonnet with silver silk under the brim and rosebuds caught at one side. The silk would lift the tone of her olive skin; and the hat would be scooped up high at the back to make the eye travel up from her shoulders and follow the line of her neck. It would draw attention to her delicate jaw, her unusual lips. The brim of the new bonnet would render Miss Thirsk's eyes even more mysterious, and Alice would await news that the woman had in train several gentlemen whose fingers ached for the smoothness of her skin. She was probably forty years old, but Alice knew that her body was sleek and glycerine beneath her clothes.

Alice had taken the shape of Miss Thirsk, the mauve and blue of her gown, the burning light of her parlour, the mystery of her—back to her worktable. She had selected a black pencil and let herself draw and draw. *Miss Thirsk,* she'd whispered, *Miss Thirsk;* so silken, so liquid, she would wash Alice away.

III

'Phrenology is useful,' John Motton was saying to himself, looking out of the window. 'It is useful, because it is true.' His father had said the same thing: it was their refrain. It had a purpose, Phrenology: to enhance the moral qualities of a person, and therefore to promote the common good. The common good—now what did that comprise these days?

Motton turned to look at his face in the mirror; he stroked his moustache, and his eyebrows. His next client would be a young man recently disgraced by his excessive gambling. John Motton patted his moustache a little more, and his beard. It was considerably bushier than his father's had been; and very black. He reached for his comb. Less gambling, for the common good—Now, who said that 'Phrenology is useful, because it is true'? It was in one of his father's journals, no doubt, perhaps the *Edinburgh Phrenological Journal*. 1840s, most certainly. He went to the cabinet, studied the yellow spines, pulled out 1842, flicked through, pulled out 1841, his eye was caught by a discussion of Combe's treatises against spicy foods and living near stagnant water. Ah, Phrenology—he turned back to the window.

His client was late, but a young woman was clattering up the steps to his front door. Pretty, yes, very pretty, though rather dishevelled—he looked more closely as she came level with the window—regular features, good proportions. She must, he thought, be his mother's new milliner. She was moving out of sight now, her hatboxes and her skirts, she was entering his house, she was outside his Room, in the dark hall, moving forward on dainty feet towards his mother. He edged to the door, and checked himself. Little milliners, all the same, with their fancy ideas and pins on

21

the Persian rugs. Pretty, pretty, pretty, though, most of them.

The young man was very late. John Motton deplored lateness. Nevertheless, he would soon cure the lad of his impropriety. He, Motton, would never be late. And gambling—gambling! What was it? Poker? The vacuous, skill-less roulette? Quite out of the question. What was important was knowledge: self-knowledge, mental discipline, self-control; the controlled exercise of the mental and moral faculties. He breathed in. Con-trol. Ah, milliners—and hats! His mother had such a penchant for hats. Since his father's death she had become a plaything of fashion, each season tossed this way and that. Dressmakers exploiting her frailty, milliners designing great cavernous bonnets that made his mother's face appear like a single piece of coal in a scuttle. Poor, stupid Mother. Poor, stupid, sweet, precious little Mother. And this new milliner, what would this pretty new miss produce?

Motton spun the miniature globe that sat on his desk. He studied the humming bird in its glass case, admiring its glistening eye. 'Law,' he murmured to himself, 'yes, that is the word. Laws. Let us establish and adhere to laws.' But first, he would scratch a few details about the milliner into his book, his first impressions. He sat down at his desk, dipped his pen, and wrote '*She is louche, even carnal. Intelligent, nevertheless, but not entirely honest. Most certainly under-nourished. And little piety.*' He would look forward to being able to match these impressions with the phrenological categories that would properly and more accurately describe the young woman, because it was only a matter of time before she would be in this Room, sitting on his special chair, whilst he observed her, and measured her, and scooped up her hair—but now he was interrupted by his client cracking at the front door with his cane—quite unnecessary. Motton smoothed his moustache once again and waited for the tap

22

at his own door, for Mary's flat vowels (that girl, so loyal, so bitter). 'Phrenology is useful, because it is true,' he whispered to himself, and opened the door.

Alice looked again at the address on the printed card: *Belinda Motton, Church Street, Kensington,* and looked up at the house. A dark-bearded man was standing at the window as Alice arrived, his form growing larger and more distinct as she climbed the steps. She clutched her skirts and hatboxes with one hand, trying to look elegant. She hoped he would reappear at the front door when she rang the bell—instead she stood before a maidservant with a large mole on her chin. But out of the corner of her eye Alice could still see him through the window, and he had turned to face her. The servant looked accusing, and Alice whispered her name. Without replying, the girl ushered Alice inside and down a narrow hallway. As Alice grew accustomed to the dark, another woman appeared; a runner bean, a crinoline on a stem.

'Ah, Miss Heapy!' Mrs. Motton clasped Alice's arm and led her into the parlour, where the two women stared at each other through a pencil of dust suspended in the morning sun. Alice began to open one of her hatboxes, becoming aware of the room: burgundy velvet, dark blue glass, screens and fringes. She turned to Mrs. Motton; two gold-lipped china dogs loomed and receded on the mantelpiece behind her.

'Well, Mrs. Motton, I have brought you some samples.'

Mrs. Motton was a little bent to the right side, Alice observed, and the joints of her wrists were swollen. She had a bony nose which, in the sunlight, was transparent around the nostrils, and her brown eyes cut tiny triangles into her face. She was fifty-eight or sixty, perhaps a little older. The bearded man was surely not her husband.

'Mrs. Zaphinov speaks highly of you, my dear.' Mrs.

Motton's voice seemed to come from her eyes.

'Thank you, ma'am.'

'Now, Miss Heapy—it has to be prune, you see, or *purée de pois*. These are the season's colours, my dear. In fact, my dressmaker is arriving this minute to measure me for a dress, rather flat at the front, with a little more fullness at the back—in *purée de pois*. The hat must therefore be *pois*, or prune, perhaps, with a low crown and an *aigrette* of gold-tinted feathers.' Mrs. Motton pronounced the French words with her eyes almost closed.

Please no, thought Alice, not prune, not pea, but she smiled and looped her measuring tape round Mrs. Motton's temples, down from the crown to the nape of the neck. The woman twitched and fidgeted. Alice put down her measuring tape and stretched her hands loosely across Mrs. Motton's forehead, letting her fingers meet. Then she placed her hands over the woman's crown, over the coil of grey and white hair, which was wispy and soft. Mrs. Motton became still, with a look of coy satisfaction. Vain, thought Alice, a vain little bird who likes to be touched, and she predicted that Mrs. Motton would try to peck her soon enough, darting forward when she was least expecting it. Alice took up her pencil and wrote down the measurements in her book, thinking she'd best not put feathers on this hat or Mrs. Motton might fly up to the eaves.

'Did you see my son, Miss Heapy? He is very fine, very handsome, don't you think?' *The man framed at the window.* 'John is a Phrenologist—and *highly* respected, as indeed was my late husband. Have you ever had your head delineated, my dear?'

'No, ma'am,' and Alice blushed because she imagined Mr. John Motton's highly respected hands roaming over her head. 'Although,' she remembered, 'I believe my father used to be interested in the practice, ma'am.'

24

'Did he, my dear? Good. Well then, bring me the designs as soon as you can, my dear, as soon as you possibly can. In the meantime I shall ask my girl Mary to bring you a sample of my new *purée de pois* and also perhaps the prune. *Mary!* Mary appeared instantly. 'Ah, show Miss Heapy out, will you.'

Mary led Alice back down the hall and past what Alice thought must be Mr. Motton's Consulting Room. As she walked down the steps, she couldn't resist looking up at his window, and indeed she saw him, the side of his big whiskered face, and his hands raised, as if in supplication.

IV

Alice was sitting at her worktable, with her note book open. She wrote:

I shall look at him through a pearl button, to change his countenance, to cast light upon him. I shall wrap his hair in a length of oyster silk, to make a woman of him. I shall fringe him with brocade, to mock him and to disguise him from myself; and this is the first day.

Then she put down her pen and made a few sketches for Mrs. Motton's hat, considering which colours would lighten the tone of her skin, what shape would broaden her narrow face, when she heard her landlady on the stairs.

'Alice Heapy,' she called up. 'You've got a *visitor.*'

Alice opened the door to find herself staring at Mary, who was clutching a loosely-wrapped paper parcel. The Motton's maidservant eased herself into Alice's room without waiting to be invited, and once inside she seemed to be a kind of magnet, sucking everything in the room into her eyes. Alice folded her arms and watched her—she was hardly a girl, perhaps thirty-five or thirty-eight, and she looked, thought Alice, as if she knew things about John Motton, things she shouldn't know, things she'd discovered by this special method of ingesting all the objects in a room. Alice blushed: perhaps Mary already knew; or if not, she would find out—Alice's note book was open on the worktable. Yes, Alice was certain. Mary already knew that she had thought John Motton handsome, that she had imagined his hands roaming on her head. But she would not have this Mary judging her, and she tried to snatch the parcel from her. Mary clutched the parcel to her chest, then with an almost imperceptible hiss, put it down on the table, opened the door herself and went out on to the landing.

When Alice heard the front door bang, she cut the string and carefully unwrapped the paper. Inside was a square of felt the colour of old prunes, and underneath, a piece of wool in a powdery green-yellow, a fine colour for mashed peas next to a pink ham. Alice put the fabrics down and began to search amongst her boxes of embroidery threads for pearl, and gold, and cranberry.

The following afternoon Alice took her designs to Mrs. Motton and this time John Motton himself opened the door as she was only half way up the steps. She found herself curtseying and blushing—ah, the shame of not being able to conceal. She would, she promised herself, rehearse for such meetings in future. She would set a plain expression in aspic before she went out of her room. But John Motton was standing before her in a tweed and leather suit; standing huge, magnificent even, like an oak tree, a great dark trunk. Now he was gesturing her inside, but as she began to move forward, he did not move at all. As she endeavoured to pass into the house, he seemed to be examining her every detail; she could hear him breathing. He would be able to hear her heart beating. She tried to see into the hallway for a sign of Mrs. Motton or the servant girl, at least, but could see nothing except John Motton's great shoulder, and her sight seemed to be impaired by the smell of the man: tobacco, a bit of starch perhaps, and something feminine, very faint, a woman's perfume.

At last John Motton ended this awkward proximity and stepped aside. 'Come, my dear,' he said, leading Alice down the dark corridor. 'Mother is out visiting friends. No doubt she will return shortly.' Alice noticed his slight lisp. 'I shall ask Mary to bring us some tea.'

Alice sat forward on the edge of her velvet chair whilst John Motton settled back in his, and as if he hadn't spent enough time intruding upon her in the doorway, he gazed at her with dark brown eyes between black eyebrows, in a most leisurely fashion. With what, thought Alice, could she possibly interest the man? He seemed quite at ease with the ensuing silence, although it must have been apparent to him that she was not. Their legs and the Universe were between them. She wished she'd worn a veil. She thought of asking him if she might crouch behind the Chinese screen in the corner while they waited. Instead, she studied the velvet cushion at her side, slowly pushing the nap first one way, and then the other. The milliner and the phrenologist remained in this arrangement until the man deigned to speak.

'Miss Alice Heapy.' He said her name and smiled, revealing a gap between his front teeth. 'Miss Alice Heapy,' he repeated, and a little air escaped.

You see how he says my name and then makes me wait.

At last, John Motton continued: 'Miss Alice Heapy, please, tell me about your trade. Do you take pleasure in your work?'

Did she take pleasure in her work? How could she possibly answer? For a second she felt committed to a Masonic secrecy and she cast about the room; a fox stared back at her from its glass case, and she had a vision of Mrs. Motton circling the room above the two of them, wanting and not wanting to be noticed.

'It is—exacting work, Sir.'

'Exacting. That sounds rather like my profession, Miss Heapy. In what way, exacting?'

Alice didn't answer immediately. She thought about Mary, with the mole on her chin and the stealing eyes, stealing all her special millinery tools, her scissors and her needles, and her buckram and willow, and bringing them to John Motton for his inspection.

'Well?' He was insistent.

28

Alice's heart was beating hard. She looked directly at the man. She thought his countenance was inquisitorial yet curiously satisfied, as if he was working through a great volume of questions to which he already knew the answers.

'I suppose I could, Sir, describe the making of a hat from the first thoughts of the design to the final fitting, but…'

His skin was sallow under his long whiskers; his black hair curled slightly over a low forehead. She noticed his large, pink earlobes. His waiting lips, waiting for his chance to ask further questions, were thick and well-formed, almost womanly in their definition. It was this feature, Alice now realised—the balance between the manly and the womanly—that rendered him handsome, similar to the balance in Miss Thirsk. But he—there was also something slightly—but no, she would not be afraid of him, she would not be afraid of a bully, or a bear, or a tree trunk.

'Yes, Miss Heapy, describe the process from your design to the fitting,' he commanded. 'Describe it to me.'

At that moment Mary appeared between them with a tray of tea. She set the tray down, glancing at each of them, and surely smirking. Then she proceeded to pour tea from a golden teapot into little blue and white cups. Alice thought this might distract John Motton from requiring her answer, but as Mary receded and the door closed, he flicked his hand towards Alice and raised his eyebrows. Alice stood up abruptly.

'First of all, I look at the lady in question,' she said, catching sight of herself in the mirror over the fireplace. He nodded in approval, rather prematurely, she thought. 'I look at the shape of her face, at her neck and her shoulders. I watch how she moves, how she carries herself, what kinds of gestures she makes.'

I feel the lady's head, I let my hands follow its lines. I feel the bone through her hair, her fine or coarse, her flat or coiled hair. Bone and

29

hair and skin. I feel the warmth radiating from her head. I consider
the shape that is made by the skull and the hair, the ears, the length
of the neck and the angles of the jaw, and I imagine the inside of the
hat first, quickly, whilst I can still feel the warmth rising up through
the bone.

'I look at the colour and the texture of her skin and her hair, and her eyes, Sir, and I wonder about her, whether she…'

He is ridiculing me, thought Alice, for there was a half-smile on John Motton's face—and a flame licked her face and throat. She sat down.

'And what of *your* profession, Sir?' But then Mrs. Motton was in the room, unpinning her cape and draping it over a chair.

'Johnny, I have seen Mrs. Zaphinov and she tells me that our little milliner here doesn't ever use straw, you know. Have you ever heard of a milliner who doesn't use straw? Whatever will my new hat be made of, dear—*bones?*'

Alice sipped at her tea, paying close attention to the pattern on the teacup, running her finger over the blue pagodas and the miniature bridges. The rim of the cup was painted gold and fluted—she couldn't place her lip quite flush at its edge, so that her lips also became fluted and she feared the tea would roll away down the tiny funnels and on to her lap. She observed the transparent surface of the tea floating above the milk.

'She *refuses* to use straw,' Mrs. Motton repeated, emitting a narrow laugh. Alice wished Mrs. Motton would not laugh, *she knew nothing about straw.*

Then John Motton was speaking, 'And why is that, Miss Heapy? It's most unusual. Intriguing.' Alice glanced up to meet his eyes as he continued. 'Why make your life more difficult than necessary—well, I presume it *is* more difficult to make hats and bonnets in a different way to every other milliner in the land?'

Alice was roused. 'Not every milliner, Sir. It is common practice to use a variety of materials and structures. Did you not see the Great Exhibition, Sir? My father took me—I was quite young—we saw hats made of every material—grasses from Cuba, palmetto leaves, Manila hemp.'

Mrs. Motton sniffed and John Motton cut in, 'Well then, Miss Heapy, it could indeed be to your commercial advantage to use your rare, possibly unique, methods and materials. But why *refuse* to use straw, if that is the case?' He looked towards his mother. Alice didn't like him making this suggestion about commercial advantage, yet in a way he was right. It was only the uniqueness of her designs that would enable her to live.

'I use willow,' she began, wanting to explain that willow was an excellent, flexible material for construction, one that she frequently used in her creations. But the word was imperfectly formed: 'Wi'wo.' She thought she could hear Mrs. Motton chirping. If only they knew what she had seen, those two, with their perfect lips, his womanly, hers tiny but complete; knew what she and Edward had witnessed, then they would not chirp and laugh and torment her. If they knew that her mother had died from a cancer that first developed in her lip, from wetting the straw, from continually wetting the straw. She stared into her cup. As she tipped the last drops of tea towards her mouth, a cluster of blue clouds edged with an arc of sunrays became visible at the bottom of the cup, and then she was saying it:

'Squamous-celled epithelioma.' Alice could not say 'willow' but she could pronounce this phrase perfectly. She looked up—Mrs. Motton had raised her handkerchief to her nose and her speck-eyes were suspicious. John Motton had his hand on his chin, his own mouth partly covered. *On her beautiful, shining lower lip, an ulcer than never healed, a crust with sharp edges, a scab as hard as a beetle, right there on my mother's lip.*

'She treated it herself at first, with nitrate of silver. She didn't know. They said it was the very worst thing she could have done. When she died, she hadn't left her room for two years.' Would Alice also say that cancer of the lip was more common than any other except for that of the tongue, and the uterus? She would certainly not say the word 'uterus'—nor 'tongue'. 'We nursed her. My brother Edward and I.' *And we were glad Father was dead and wouldn't see her like this. Although in the end she forgot he was dead, she said he was just outside the door, that he was too discreet to come in, that he did not want to shame her.* 'It spread, you see, and she had to have the tumour cut away, but it was in her jaw bone, and if she had lived she would have lost part of her cheek, and both her lips. Because of the straw, Sir.'

Of course, it was too intimate. John Motton rose from his chair. He bowed and excused himself, brushing past Alice on his way to the door. Mary came in and noisily cleared away the cups.

Alice laid out her drawings and fabric samples on the low table. Mrs. Motton clapped her hands. She chose a design for a hat in cranberry silk. She did not notice it was neither prune nor *purée de pois* and she did not inquire about the missing *aigrette* of tinted feathers. The dressmaker would arrive this minute to measure Mrs. Motton for a dress in cranberry silk.

V

Alice decided to look kindly on the Mottons' rudeness, putting it down to their class. And the following day, she was able to enjoy a little ridicule of her own. As she was passing the tea rooms on her way to look at some new aniline dyes, she noticed John Motton sitting at one of the tables, partly obscured from her by a pillar. She could see that he had a book open next to his plate. He hadn't seen her, and she moved back slightly so that she could watch him without being noticed. He was chewing what was probably some kind of meat sandwich, and it amused Alice to see his jawbones moving in large, regular circles. She could see his smooth temples becoming red and crinkly-veined, how his whiskery cheek hollowed and puffed, how the chin first elongated and then flattened out. The little dent under his nose spread and puckered, spread and puckered, and Alice couldn't take her eyes off him, for it seemed that he was never going to take a fresh bite. He probably needed to spit out some offending gristle, but he didn't, and Alice waited and waited; and neither did he swallow. Then he looked over to where she was standing, and she decided it was time to get on with her errand.

John Motton finally decided to summon the waitress. 'Gristle,' he said. 'There is gristle in my sandwich.'

The girl darted off with the offending item, and Motton closed his book, *The Illustrated Self-Instructor in Phrenology, Physiology, and Physiognomy* by the American, Lorenzo Fowler. It was he who was the gristle in the sandwich. A mere entertainer, a disgrace to the profession. He would be the nail in the coffin for scientific phrenology, and he was right here in London, established in his own Institute at Ludgate Circus. Motton stroked his beard. He would write a paper for the *Journal*. He began to sketch out the article in his mind, and, turning towards the light outside, saw Alice Heapy, watching him. No doubt she imagined she was invisible—ah, now she was invisible, the furtive, secretive little thing. Yet he couldn't help but admire her treatise on her mother's disease yesterday, and he was most interested in how she studied her clients before she formulated her designs. How similar it was to his own analysis of the human propensities and form, except, of course, that her approach was not at all scientific. She used the methods of all artisans, taking what he might describe as an 'impressionistic' view, without the benefit of categories or principles or Laws; and, of course, without any moral purpose. Her work was, therefore, frivolous. Yes, he thought, her talents were wasted on frivolity. Yet it pleased his mother, and what pleased his mother should please him, for it meant that she might not complain or ask him to fetch her gloves or her cribbage or her fashion newspaper. Fashion, at her age.

Motton calculated that the girl had rather too little *Veneration*, a common fault in young milliners today, in any artisans—far too little respect for their superiors. He considered, too, that there was a little *Destructiveness*, but the *Perceptive* organs—they were very well developed. And yes, she was indeed pretty: the sweep of wavy hair, the petticoat of eyelashes, the well-defined lips, the fine, rising forehead. She reminded him of someone—yes, in this she distinctly reminded him of someone.

The manager appeared, proffering a new sandwich and flourishing a fresh burgundy napkin across John Motton's stomach. The manager bowed, and John Motton nodded, still thinking of the little milliner, her big eyes and her pointed nose and chin, and the very daintiness of her bones; thought of her peeping at him whilst he minded his own business in the tea rooms, watching him eat his gristly sandwich—spying on him. John Motton brought the napkin up to his forehead as it dawned on him that the 'Little Milliner' thought him probably rather fine. He smiled to himself, and proceeded to reconsider the problem of Mister Fowler. Yes, he would definitely write a paper for the *Journal*, and the title would be 'Fowler's side-show phrenology' with the sub-title 'The case for the *scientific* Phrenology of Dr. George Combe.' Or was it *Mr.* Combe? He sincerely hoped it was *Dr.*

Alice prepared for her next visit to the Mottons by stretching her hair into a tight knot and stepping into her drabbest dress, the charcoal one that was threadbare under the arms. This time she would be stern; she would practice stern in the mirror, and she would relinquish any bid for elegance. She set out with giant strides towards Church Street.

But when Alice was dressing she had forgotten that the weather this autumn was proving to be most un-seasonal, and the sun beat mercilessly on her dark dress. By the time she had got as far as Madame D'Acier's in Silver Street she was sweating and flushed. She scurried past the shop praying that Madame wouldn't, at this particular moment, be adjusting the window display with pins in her mouth, and she wasn't. Alice had so very recently escaped Madame's exacting tutelage. It was only a few months since she had been forced to listen to her daily lectures on Taste, which the woman defined as '*Une harmonie, un accord de l'esprit et de la raison.*' Every day of Alice's apprenticeship Madame had repeated, in her nasal whine, the philosophy of Edmund Burke: '*It is known that the taste is improved exactly as we improve our judgements—by extending our knowledge, by a steady attention to our object, and by frequent exercise.*'

Yes, thought Alice, she would pay a steady attention to her object: not Mrs. Motton, but her son, John Motton.

She would return his leisurely gaze; she would ask him questions to which she already knew the answers; she would brush past him, drawing in the smell of him; and all the while she would delight him with her ingenuity, and with her exquisite taste, and her fine artistry.

Just as Alice was crossing towards the Mottons' house, she was deafened by the noise of scraping hooves and men roaring. She managed to cover her face with her arm as she was pushed up against the railings by the wet flanks of a Cavalry horse. When light returned she saw the rider, having gained control, waving down at her. 'Ma'am!' Alice's drab was now torn and dusty as well as perished. She tasted linseed oil, leather, and dung. As she was recovering she glanced up to see John Motton at his window, not smiling openly, but certainly amused.

Alice hesitated, she attempted to brush down her skirts and pat her hair. She considered turning back, and missing her appointment. But she was expecting to be paid for her designs today, and John Motton had already seen her. She breathed in deeply, marched up the steps and vigorously pulled at the doorbell. Mary opened the door a fraction, her finger pressed accusingly to her lips. She whispered that Alice was to tread quietly because Mr. Motton was *doing a head-reading*. As she tiptoed past John Motton's hallowed Consulting Room, Alice strained to detect his voice, perhaps delivering judgement upon some poor sweet head, but she could hear nothing at all except her own boots meeting the floor tiles.

Still shaken by her ordeal with the horse, Alice could barely concentrate on Mrs. Motton's fitting, and anyway she was also trying to imagine exactly what it was that John Motton did in that Room. But just as she began to despair of her lack of will, or was it wilfulness, she caught a glimpse of how the style of the hat gave Mrs. Motton a new, balanced shape. She was no longer a bean pod. The cranberry hat really had given her a new dignity. Mrs. Motton noticed Alice's change of countenance.

'How does it look, Miss Heapy? Is the shape very becoming?' Mrs. Motton looked in the mirror over the fireplace; she twisted and pouted, she put her hands on her hips.

'Yes, Mrs. Motton, it suits you. The height of the cap is perfect, and that narrow brim. And see how the satin underneath the brim casts a beautiful light on to your face.'

Alice's hat gave the illusion that Mrs. Motton's thin nose had broadened a little; the discreetly reduced brim brought harmony to the woman's face; even the tiny eyes were magnified, and now they filled with tears.

'Ah, ah, Miss Heapy. Ah! I think we can work well together, yes. My dear girl. *Johnny! Joh-n-ee!'*

'Oh Mrs. Motton,' Alice put a finger to her lips, 'your maid said we must be very quiet, that Mr. Motton is *doing a head-reading.'*

'Bother, my dear. Now listen: I have *occasions* throughout the winter, for which I must have the best outfits. You must work with my dressmaker, she also sews for Mrs. Haviland you know, and she is most upset, Miss Heapy, that I engaged you without first having formal discussions with her. She says, my dear, that milliners and dressmakers should always work together on an outfit, but then I had you on the recommendation of Mrs. Zaphinov, after all, and you know that her late father was a Member of Parliament, don't you? *John-nee!'*

'Mrs. Motton! We must be quiet.' *So now I am John Motton's guardian.*

'Oh, it's all right, I can hear him now, Miss Heapy, he has finished. Listen.'

John Motton's voice was solicitous, and it partnered a woman's voice. Alice tried to listen but Mrs. Motton was also speaking, her voice becoming increasingly shrill.

'Yes, I shall have an entirely new wardrobe, full of cranberry and pearl, and perhaps some French yellows—gorse, perhaps.' *Please, not gorse.* Mrs. Motton caught sight of herself again in the mirror; she was still wearing the hat, which was dabbed with pins, 'Ah, thank you, my dear, thank you. *Johnny!*'

'No, Mrs. Motton—don't let him see it yet—he can see it when it's finished. Let it be our secret until it's finished.'

'Well, let us have Mary in here at least. *Mary!*'

Mary must have been waiting right outside the door because she was in the room almost before Mrs. Motton had said the second syllable of her name.

'Look at me, Mary, look at Miss Heapy's little miracle.'

Mary cast her omnivorous eye over Alice Heapy. Alice stared back at Mary, but then Mary let her eyes rest on her so long that Alice's hand reached involuntarily up to her jaw. Then John Motton was in the room, altering the light, smiling indulgently at his mother and taking her hands into his. He was larger than Alice remembered even though she had seen him so recently; and she could smell, definitely, a woman's perfume: jasmine. As he turned towards her she noticed a tension in the man's upper lip, so that she found herself curtseying and trying to smooth the mud off her skirts. Yes, she needed to be invisible before him, yet she also wanted his gaze upon her. She was aroused against her will.

Mother was calling him. Always calling. This afternoon, for example: 'Johnny! Johnny darling!'—calling in the special high voice she always used to summon him. He felt his chest tighten as he put down his newspaper, so he picked up the newspaper again and carried on reading until she called again. At last he walked slowly through to the back parlour where she was waiting, dressed for visiting.

'Fetch my gloves, Johnny dear, they're on the hall stand.'

38

'Mother, are you not going in that direction, right past the hall stand, on your way out of the front door? Could you not collect your gloves, on the way past, dear Mother?'

'Indeed I could, dear boy, but first I wish to try them against this cape, in this mirror here by the window. If you would just—the bronze leather ones.'

John fetched the gloves. He rubbed them between his thumb and forefinger; they were worn and smooth, like a woman's earlobe. He laid the gloves on his mother's lap. She eased her fingers into the gloves.

He said, almost fondly, 'Mother, this is your last chance to be exasperating, because tomorrow I am working on my paper for the *Phrenological Review* challenging the latest— what shall I call them—the latest *perambulations* of Mister Alexander Bain, and then a lighter piece for the *Journal* on that American fool over at Ludgate Circus, and I cannot be interrupted at all. *At all.* Not for the fetching of gloves, not for distraught clients, not for...' He nearly said 'Not even for pretty milliners.' 'Not for anyone.'

'You are so very clever, my dear,' said his mother, slipping off the gloves.

John Motton went back to his room and once again took up the newspaper. It was the *Kensington Gazette*. He was reading with disbelief about packs of wild dogs up at St. John's and St. James' when his mother began calling him again. John Motton folded his paper and put it on the side table. He continued to sit. Then he took the newspaper and folded it again, folded it until it was almost the size of an envelope. He cast around for a paperweight, none to be seen. So he took his spectacles case and smoothed the edges of the newspaper, over and over.

'Johnny!'

Mother was still sitting in her chair by the window. 'Darling, could you possibly fetch me the other gloves, the azure ones, Johnny, they're in my bedroom, on the dressing table. I am sorry, but you know it's Mary's afternoon off. The azure ones with the gold buttons to the side.'

John Motton trod slowly upstairs, tapping his knuckles against the mahogany balustrade. At the top of the stairs he surveyed the landscapes on the landing wall, noticing dust on the frames. He got out his handkerchief and began to blow and polish. Then he went to the dressing table in his mother's room, sat on the stool, studied himself in the mirrors, only after some minutes had passed finally snatching up the gloves: the azure ones with the gold buttons to the side.

Belinda Motton smiled up at him, triumphant. He longed for her to leave.

'Let me escort you to the carriage, my dear mother.'

The two moved forward, Belinda's arm tucked in to his; he felt fur on the globes of his eyes. But with Mother out visiting and Mary's afternoon off, he could think about her, Isabella—think about Mrs. Isabella Raleigh's knees, and her calves; recall the fragrance of her.

He is already warm, aroused, as he walks with his mother down the steps to the carriage, helping her in, closing the door gently, kissing his mother's cheek through the open window, waving to her, calling to her to take good care on her journey. Now he retraces his steps and inside leans with his back against the heavy front door. He thinks of Mrs. Isabella Raleigh, who he pays four guineas just to gaze at her naked white skin; forcing himself to stare at her, aroused almost to distraction but never touching her. He places his hand lightly over his groin, leaning against the front door, alone in the house, without his mother calling and without Mary listening at the bottom of the cellar stairs.

VI

Alice had rushed away from the Mottons' without her payment. She would remain cold and hungry. It was a beautiful chance therefore that she arrived home to find a card from Miss Thirsk, asking Alice to visit her that evening. Those sculpted lips and that swan neck would arrest, would wash away the mark of that Motton household; Alice would be warm; and Miss Thirsk had, said her note, some news.

They sat, as usual, close to the fire, Miss Thirsk wrapped round in rose-printed silk. She had, she said, in recent weeks, drawn a gentleman towards her—a short, rotund gentleman. She had been walking in parks with him; she had listened closely with him in Lecture Halls. It was just as Alice had imagined: a bulbous man who needed to stretch himself up to reach her; and now Miss Thirsk said to Alice that her *beau*, if a short, round gentleman may be called a *beau*, had proposed to her. So she would need dresses and hats for both her imminent wedding and her honeymoon.

'He desires that I wear a lilac dress,' she said. 'He brings me lavender perfume, and flowers, winter violets. And Alice, he kisses my hand, and continues kissing all along my arm.'

'Then I shall make a hat that will astound this romantic man,' said Alice as colours and shapes formed in her head: lavender, violets, kisses that traced a woman's arm.

Miss Thirsk ran her fingers along a row of ginger jars and then, with her long neck, leant towards Alice and whispered, 'Rapture—the other women, they were all in a state of rapture. It was dusk, the lamps were lit, and they were wearing long floral robes and had their hair loose to their waists. They were listening to the poet, Algernon Charles Swinburne, and in the listening their bodies lent themselves to the poem, theirs whose *'languid lips are sweeter/Than love's who fears to greet her'*. Last week I attended another Reading, I watched the women's faces, I hoped to move into that rapturous state myself. I kept my mouth closed, though softly, and I kept my eyes open, though gently, and waited to be taken by the poems. But I did not, I could not, I could not allow myself to drift away as they did. It is my sadness, Alice, it keeps the world away from me, keeps it behind a little veil. I can see the world only through fine mesh.

'Of course, the gentlemen always know it is there. They bring their plump fingers up to stroke my face and the veil stops them, one quarter of an inch away from my skin. One quarter of an inch! You would think I had measured the distance. You know, Alice,' Miss Thirsk leant closer to Alice, 'I loved a gentleman once, and he loved me, I am sure of it, but he never said. He visited and went away, on perhaps ten or twelve occasions, and each time he went away, he took a little of my veil with him, until by the final visit I was glowing free of the mesh. But he never returned. So now I keep that veil on, Alice, for the men with the plump fingers.'

It was also what Alice wanted: her spinster-bride veil.

Miss Thirsk said that at her wedding she should like to conceal herself beneath a hooded shoulder cape, a kind of Eastern bashlik. Indeed she wished to be doubly concealed, for under the hood she wanted a veil made from the finest Chinese silk chain-mail, stained with blackcurrants, as if etched over her face. Perhaps, thought Alice, she could make the veil from a *mousseline de soie*. Yes, Miss Thirsk's gentleman would have the pleasure of seeking out his bride through the mesh, slowly finding her smooth neck warm inside the bashlik.

Alice stroked Miss Thirsk's hair. They tipped their heads together. For Alice to imagine, to conceive of, tirelessly to breathe life into this woman's wedding costume thus was also to *marry* her: let the husband show Alice the difference between her special attentions and his.

In her threadbare dress and cloak Alice ran home from Miss Thirsk's. A terrible smell hung in the stillness of the night air. The man at the bookstall said it was the pigs at Notting Hill, another said it was the Gas Works. Alice wrapped her arms round herself. She had a secret: she loved a woman and a man. She loved a woman and a man and her heart could encompass the world.

But in her room this night, plain became bare; her cupboard contained one slice of salt beef and half an apple. Alice put her mother's tartan over her head and sucked on the salt beef. She should have asked Miss Thirsk for an advance, for how was she to purchase a little coal, let alone the expensive *mousseline de soie*? Perhaps Nash's would give her credit if she would agree to take on some repairs. If not, she would be found, a rigid corpse, upright at her work table, her fingers locked in sewing position. She sat down at once to write out a bill addressed to Mrs. Belinda Motton, knowing that she would have to work all night to finish the hat if she wanted to be paid for it tomorrow. She wrote out the bill, and her notebook was still open on the desk, so she wrote in it, 'John Motton, *my darling*' to tease. Then a dull boom passed through her chest and a white light flashed across her window. Shortly after, she heard Mrs. Peake on the stairs, treading up and down, tapping on each of her lodgers' doors and shouting, 'Gas Works! They say it's the Gas Works.'

In the night, as she made each of the tiny stitches into the cranberry silk, Alice tried to think kindly of Mrs. Belinda Motton and her son, for she was Mrs. Motton's milliner; and Mrs. Motton had been pleased with her designs. She needed to care a little less about Mary's

strangeness and about John Motton's—what? Man-ness?
Madame D'Acier would say she simply needed to be a little
more professional. Nevertheless, by three o'clock that
morning, she had made a cartoon sketch of the man, at his
window, his beard and eyebrows obscuring most of his
face, and the hat wasn't finished until seven.

At half past nine that morning Alice delivered the finished
hat to Mrs. Motton. Alice had her purse in her hand, which
now contained two guineas. She might have two glasses of
beer with Edward at The Civet Cat that evening, and buy a
piece of mustard ham as well as the coal.

Mary led Alice to the front door, but the door of John
Motton's Consulting Room was open. She peeped inside:
no Motton. Mary was opening the front door, she was
waving to someone, and Alice edged inside the Room, her
heart beating in her ears. The first thing she saw was a glass
cabinet containing a bird—it was a humming bird; its long
beak was almost the same length as its round body. Along
one wall was a row of bookcases; and on the walnut and
leather desk stood a porcelain phrenological head, etched
into distinct sections. She crossed the Room towards the
head. Lined up next to the inkwell were two sets of brass
callipers, similar to her own, but rather more beautiful. Her
fingers reached towards the callipers, she thought she
might recognise the name of the manufacturer, but then
the floor was creaking behind her.

'*Miss Heapy!*'

John Motton was very close; down to her left she could
see his intricately-embossed chestnut leather shoe alongside
her grey silk boot. She thought perhaps he had been eating
crystallized ginger and she could also smell camphor, and
something else, something she could not name. She could
feel the fibres of his herringbone jacket, and the coldness
of leather. Again '*Miss Heapy!*' His breath was on her neck;

his voice, with its wisp of air through the teeth, speaking her name, and she was aware of the outline of her shoulders, of her corset nipping at her waist.

'Excuse me, Sir, I...'

'Allow me to *show* you my Consulting Room, Madam. Why don't you sit down?'

Alice followed the line of the Phrenologist's outstretched hand towards a chair opposite the desk. Motton moved behind the desk and gestured to the porcelain head, which stood, severed just above the shoulders, on a circle of brass. Alice could see now that each section was engraved over with a word, words that already seemed familiar: *Amativeness, Combativeness, Veneration.* Motton placed his hands on the head and revolved it slowly, all the time with his eyes on Alice, pronouncing the names of each of the Faculties, proudly, as if he had invented them that very moment.

He pointed up at his collection of medical and philosophical books on the shelves behind him, to the bronze bust under the window. He sat down, leaning back into the deeply-buttoned chair. Alice presumed he was looking at her as she kept her eyes trained on the phrenological head. After some moments he raised himself up and brought his right hand up in a beckoning motion. 'Well, Miss Heapy, I expect you would like to ask me one or two questions?'

Alice might indeed have some questions, but now, perversely, she thought about the glove cleaner who, according to Mrs. Peake, had last week died from an overdose of essential oil of almonds. 'Miss Heapy, let me explain a little.' How much almond oil did it take to kill a man? Had the man's wife poisoned him? Or was it in the course of his glove cleaning work—Motton's breathing was faster. He pointed once more to the bust near the window. 'My father was a disciple of the Viennese physician, Dr.

Franz Gall, the founder of the science, who first discovered that there are distinct organs or Faculties in the brain. Now, according to Gall, since the skull ossifies over the brain during an infant's development, the strength of each organ is manifest in the size of the bump on the skull that lies directly over that organ. What is significant, however, is not in fact the size of the individual Faculties, my dear,' he leant forward now, 'but the *pattern* of their relationship. It is this pattern that determines character and *that* can only be discerned by a skilful and experienced Phrenologist, such as myself or my father before me.'

Alice thought of her ladies: Miss Thirsk, so strange, so sensuous; Mrs. Zaphinov, a big, theatrical lion. And she imagined now that her own character was a flexible, elastic thing, for right this minute, in its relation to Mr. John Motton, she would describe herself as contrary: on the one hand competitive, wanting to assert the superiority of her own work, and on the other hand, she felt, to her surprise, hungry for *his* knowledge—this idea of the 'pattern of the relationship' between the Faculties, for example, and she felt hungry, for some raw thing—But Motton was giving his Lecture, his hand placed now on top of a pile of papers:

'Miss Heapy,' he continued, 'my father was closely acquainted with someone I am sure you will have heard of, the great Scottish Phrenologist George Combe, who, by his system of Moral Philosophy, worked to understand how each of us is but an assemblage of contradictions, of competing energies which are themselves determined by the strengths and weaknesses of the individual Faculties.

'Now, I have been studying faces since the age of eight, when my father and I would go out to the hotels to compare the physiognomies of the guests with those of the staff: to witness how good breeding determined the facial features, the height of the brow, for example. And not much later, under the direction of my father, of course, I was reading the enlightened and brilliant early scientific Phrenologists, Gall, as I mentioned, and Spurzheim—then, and this was a great experience of my early life, I attended the Lecture by the great Dr. George Combe, here at the London Institute. There were hundreds in the audience. Not long after that Lecture my father began to train me so that I could continue his mission: to work tirelessly for the self-improvement of all. It was what the country needed; across each of the social classes. Self-improvement. And here—and here we come to the most important point, my dear.'

Now Motton walked round to Alice's side of the desk and took her hand. Alice blushed. *He is holding my hand.* At first she tried to ease her hand out of his, but he feigned not to notice, and continued on his trajectory. 'It was Combe's belief that human beings have been *adapted to virtue*, and are therefore always capable of improvement, capable of enhancing their strengths and minimizing their weaknesses, with the goal, Miss Heapy,' and now he brought his great face down to hers, 'with the goal of— *perfection*. As Combe says, indeed, the original constitution of man *is perfection*. Now, let me explain exactly: look at the Faculties on this head here. Come on, my dear, stand up so that you can see them.'

. Alice reluctantly stood up. One part of her wanted to understand the principles by which Motton worked; another part felt certain that if Phrenology's business was *correction*, then it was profoundly wrong. It was accusatory, punitive; it could only proceed by intruding on a person's privateness.

'Now, as I was saying, we are talking about the possibility of human perfection, Miss Heapy, what you desire for yourself, no doubt, and more particularly, what you desire when you design your pretty hats.' *See how he flatters me.* 'So, come now, please—listen a little longer.

47

Each of the Faculties within the human mind has a normal action. That normal action fulfilled is perfection. Any abnormal action is imperfection, and each of the Faculties should thus be cultivated by supplying each with its proper aliment. All the Faculties must be brought into harmonious concert with each other so that each of us, and the whole of society, may live perfect lives. Don't you find that a most attractive idea, Miss Heapy?'

'I am sure I do not know, Sir—and I realise that your profession is indeed very different to mine.' And she waited for him to say *'Trade, Madam. Yours is surely a trade.'* Yet he spoke gently:

'*Is* it so different, Miss Heapy? Don't *you* analyse and judge character when you design a hat? You told me yourself how you study a woman, how you consider the way she moves, how you notice the gestures she makes. Did you not ask questions about the nature and disposition of my mother? Phrenology is, after all, but a secular method of leading people towards that which is good within them: by your skilful millinery, with your first creation, you have given Mother new life—by your artistic skill *and* by your perceptive analysis of her character and her gentle spirit.'

Alice blushed again. 'I did not analyse her, Sir,' she said, as if it would be a disgrace to do so, but mainly because she was not sure that Mrs. Motton did have a gentle spirit. And she had not analysed Mrs. Motton: she had merely looked at her. She had felt a little fear at first, but when she measured her, Mrs. Motton had held out something which, unknown even to Alice at that moment, she had taken away and kept whilst she made the woman a cranberry silk hat with a light satin under-brim. But perhaps it *was* her gentle spirit, the spirit trapped beneath the woman's—what? Beneath her *imperfections*? No—it was a question of light and shape, of choosing the right colour; it was simply a question of paying *a steady attention to her object.*

Motton picked up a measuring tape now and wrapped it round the porcelain head, just above the eyes. 'I find, Alice,' he breathed, 'that people are comforted by the classification of their Faculties and qualities.' *See how he manoeuvres, now calling me Alice.* 'Indeed, they are often surprised and charmed by the prognosis. You, Alice, for example, I am sure I would find that you have a large organ of *Ideality* beating away under your curly hair. *Ideality* —it is the Faculty which is said to give us a love of the beautiful and the splendid, a desire for excellence, poetic feeling. Here—' He touched the side of the porcelain head between the temple and the crown. *In a moment he will be asking, will Miss* Alice *not submit to delineation?* 'Now then, Alice, allow me to show you the *pièce de resistance* of my profession—the callipers.'

Alice looked down at the row of brass callipers. 'Yes, Sir, I was admiring those when you came in.'

'Good—but I have another set I would like you to see.' Motton opened a draw in the desk and brought out a purple leather case. 'Come round to this side of the desk, Alice. Come. Just look at these, my dear Alice, look at these.'

Alice could see, inside the case, nestling in red plush velvet, three shining arcs of silver. John Motton lifted each of the two 'legs' out of their mouldings and placed a tiny screw in the hinge. Next he fitted the scale arm across the two legs, and held the instrument in front of Alice's face. Alice took a step backwards but Motton's eyes continued to travel over her and he began to adjust the scale arm to the width of her head. She turned away from him.

'You have nothing to fear, Miss Heapy, I have neither rack nor surgeon's knife.'

And should you wish to stretch me or make an incision in my flesh, Sir, you would not need either: you could do it with your gaze. Ah, for invisibility, for never having existed within the optical range of Mr. John Motton.

Alice was already taking up her basket and edging towards the door. 'Excuse me, Sir, but I have another appointment.' As she turned she noticed, in a glass cabinet, a collection of miniature ivory legs—ladies' legs. Two had lacy stocking tops etched into the thigh; another was clad in a thigh-boot. The legs, in ones rather than pairs, appeared to have no function; they were purely and lasciviously ornamental. So, thought Alice as she slipped out into the hallway and down on to the street, John Motton, Phrenologist, collects miniature ladies' legs, made from ivory, and she couldn't help laughing, then, and again as she sat over her fire toasting bread and eating a large slice of mustard ham.

As soon as Alice had left the Room, John Motton unlocked the glass cabinet and took out his favourite leg, the one wearing the thigh-boot: beautifully carved; exceptional craftsmanship. He took all the legs out now and placed them on a chair. He wiped the shelf with the handkerchief from his pocket, and as he did so, the image of Mrs. Isabella Raleigh rose once again, her long thighs, the porcelain buttocks. He picked up each of the legs and polished them, wrapping the cloth round the leg, smoothing and rubbing. Yes, he had frightened Alice Heapy, as she was snooping about in his private Consulting Room. Perhaps he needed to frighten her a little more, for she had barely looked up as he showed her his collection of books, as he'd demonstrated the parts of the phrenological head. She needed to be taught *Veneration,* that milliner.

He picked up several of the ivory legs from the chair, hesitating for a moment, then replaced them in what he considered to be ascending order of perfection, one behind the other, in a kind of 'evolutionary procession'. He felt rather pleased with his display, and carefully closed and locked the cabinet.

It amused him to watch his clients' reaction to his collection. He knew it was provocative, he knew Mother would rather he kept the cabinet upstairs, but he so enjoyed watching the ladies raise their hands daintily to their mouths when they realised what they were looking at. Miss Alice Heapy, for example, had registered surprise; her lips had opened and closed shut, and she had probably risen in her own estimation on account of *his* owning a collection of ladies' legs. It amused him greatly and he calculated that, surprising though it might seem, it brought him a step nearer to her agreeing to analysis.

Motton sat down at his desk. He would make a few more notes about Miss Alice Heapy before he could forget: wilful, *Combative*, with a love of *Approbation*. *Approbation*, *Combativeness, Secretiveness*. She had made him wait for her reply to his questions. He had watched her large eyes roam about the Room, move in every direction rather than look directly at him. Yes, 'large eyes', he wrote; 'forgets nothing that she sees'. Just like my maidservant, he thought. Yes, I need to teach her a little respectfulness, teach Miss Alice Heapy a little *Veneration*.

VII

There it was, surrounded by the lacy trimmings that would grace Mrs. Zaphinov's next bonnet: Lorenzo Fowler's little blue *Self-Instructor in Phrenology and Physiology—with Chart and Character*. Alice had snatched it up in Blackwell's that morning, thinking of Edward and Mother. She was certain they'd had a very similar book at home, years ago, when she was a child. As she was paying for it, the bookseller had said to her, 'Just in, that one, ma'am, it's the American fellow, new edition. We've been selling them like hot cakes yesterday and this morning.' And Alice turned to see, indeed, two women right behind her with the same book in their hands.

This was the book that defined the 'mental faculties', the one that said straight away: *'the brain is the physical organ through which the mind manifests itself.'* Alice liked the idea of the mind *manifesting* itself. But this little book wasn't really about the mind *per se*, it was about how one could know one's own and other people's characters, and, moreover, how one could *perfect* one's character and thus arrive at one's proper destination: happiness, for the common good.

Now, thought Alice, let me get this clear: the character is determined by the physical propensities of the brain, as expressed in the configuration of the skull. Yet we can alter that character by changing our behaviour. It should make sense, but—does the skull form itself *around* the brain, or does the skull *determine* the size and functioning of the brain? And if we improve our character, then won't our skulls have to shrink or stretch to accommodate the new propensities?

Alice saw that the book was also about how one could recognise an imperfect person before they had a chance to do harm, just by *Getting to Know the Organs*. Was she safe with her own ladies, for example: Mrs. Zaphinov with her great raging lion's head, or Mrs. Motton with her flat-topped bird's head? And what was she to make of the way Mrs. Zaphinov's hair sprang away from her scalp, or the way Mrs. Motton's lay down forlornly on her scalp? Of how some ladies coiled their hair into spaniels' ears, or swept it up from their brows and looped it down to their waists like Princess Eugénie of France? Did the mind not manifest itself, rather, in the precise angle at which a lady's hair sprouted forth from her head? Alice could feel a rival system of classification forming.

Why bother with Phrenology at all when a hat might conceal an imperfection? Indeed, the right hat might even *correct* that imperfection, might alter a lady's entire perception of the world. Alice realised that she did not know what rightly constituted an 'imperfection'—that was John Motton's business, to know all about the frailties and weaknesses of human nature, to carefully locate them in their special configuration in each and every person, and to trounce them.

But now she had the *Instructions*, perhaps the very ones from which Mr. John Motton worked. It amused her to see the book amongst the lacy trimmings; she adjusted them a little, to decorate.

Then her eye caught the word 'milliner'—it was on a page about the faculty of *Constructiveness:* 'If the perceptive Faculties are strong, you would make a good mechanician. If you have artistic taste, you would do well as an architect, or, if a woman, as a high-class milliner or dressmaker.'

Indeed!

Alice looked at the 'Key to the Phrenological Organs'. Apparently *Constructiveness* was situated just behind her temple, both on the right and the left side of her head. She ran her fingers over these regions. She brought her looking-glass towards her. There did indeed seem to be a slight swelling there.

Then she returned to the very first faculty: '*Amativeness.* Sexuality; the Love element; attachment to the opposite sex; desire to love, be loved, and marry.' Fowler said one may possess *Amativeness,* or indeed any of the other forty-one Faculties or organs in an amount from nought to the seventh degree, depending simply on the physical prominence of the corresponding section of the skull. This Love faculty was, apparently, situated at the base of the skull. Alice felt the place on the back of her own head - the region was remarkably flat. Perhaps, she thought, 'prominence' could also mean broad and smooth, rather than raised and bulbous. And if not, *if not,* could a Phrenologist conclude that she had no capacity for love, no sensual feeling, and therefore that she should never— marry? Alice shut the book and stood up. She covered the book with a piece of felt, and some brown paper, she put a box of buttons on top of it. She would live purely for her hats. She would live purely.

She lay down on her bed. John Motton. John Motton. Hadn't he moved round her so that he could get a glimpse of her head in profile, all the time calculating, trying to estimate the proportions of the base of her skull, trying to see under her hat, wishing her bald, perhaps? Or maybe he didn't even need to look. Maybe he had already judged her, placing her quite at the other end of the *Amativeness* scale, even allocating to her—how did Fowler put it—she took up the little book once more—here it was: 'a perversity that depraved all her other propensities', a perversity *in the seventh degree* that caused her *to treat the opposite sex solely and wantonly as a minister to passion.* Next time she visited he would exhort her to engage in some pursuit that would occupy her mind and spirit and thereby extinguish that passion—whilst hoping at the same time that she would be quite unable to restrain herself if he were to—

No—the back of Alice's head might be flat or round but she herself should nevertheless coolly place herself in the *third* degree, wherein, she read: '*You think little of the opposite sex, and are little influenced by them*'. After all, the reason she was affected by John Motton was not simply because he was a man, not simply because of his moderately good looks, but because there was something— he was concealing something important. Yes, he was concealing something, and at the same time, therefore, he was concealed from her—and yet he seemed familiar: it was as if *she* was concealed within him. Ah, this book on Phrenology! She got up from the bed. She would return at once to her patterns and blocks, she would listen to the roar of scissors cutting through taffeta, she would—she would make a *hat* for *Amativeness,* a silk swirl in the new French scarlet, lined with the creamiest, purest satin.

Or, she would analyse John Motton himself. She would divide his whole man-body into sections, but instead of renaming the parts, she would let the original names remain. She pulled out some brown pattern paper, sat down at her table and began to draw—and there he was again, John Motton, with his ears clearly marked out and separated by dotted lines from the other parts of his head. She let her eyes rest on the ears. What was it, precisely, that these ears revealed about John Motton's moral character? But this was Physiognomy, Alice realised, not Phrenology, and she remembered something Motton had said, and that she had just read in the blue book—that one must consider the size of any individual part only *in relation to* other parts. She would also consider the shape and thickness of the part, the colour and the texture of the skin, the precise *placing*—of the ear in relation to, for example, the angle of the jaw.

Alice ran her finger over the paper, tracing the imaginary ear, imagining the velvet flesh of the human ear, and the jaw. She moved the paper out of reach.

She would finish stitching gauze into ruffles, in anticipation of her visit to Mrs Zaphinov, and only then allow herself to take up the little blue book again. When she did so she studied Faculty number twenty-six: *Size, measuring by the eye.* This faculty was placed, of course, directly over the eyes. '*Cognizance of bulk, magnitude, quantity, proportion….Adapted to the absolute and relative magnitude of things. Perverted, it is pained by disproportion and architectural inaccuracies.*'

Perhaps, thought Alice, that was what was the matter with poor Edward all that time, getting laid off again and again—cutting all that sycamore and lime into the wrong thicknesses, getting the wrong measurements on the curves. He shouldn't be a hat block maker: he should have been a teacher or a clerk.

Now Alice wrote the letter to her brother.

Dearest Edward,

I have been reading a book on Phrenology. It is by Mr. Lorenzo Fowler, of the Ludgate Institute. It is because I am making hats for the mother of a Phrenologist here in Kensington—I understand he is quite eminent in the field. I am certain we had a book on the Phrenological faculties at home—do you remember it? I think it had a red cover. Do you know anything about the subject?

Mr. John Motton says that it is a Science which has greatly helped our understanding of Human Nature, but whenever I read about each of the faculties, about 'Constructiveness', for example, I do not know exactly how my understanding is enhanced. For under this heading, all it says is: 'If the perceptive faculties are strong, you would make a good mechanician. If you have artistic taste, you would do well as an architect, or, if a woman, as a high-class milliner or dressmaker'. *You see, Edward, I read and*

*read but I cannot tell whether I am at the start or the end of my
journey. This, when I should be contemplating the difference between
gauze and French tulle, between Chinese and Valenciennes lace. Let
us meet on Thursday evening, Edward, six o'clock in The Civet Cat
(I've just been paid two guineas). You can tell me then what you know
about Phrenology.*

*With affection, and regards to Cassandra—
your sister, Alice.'*

Alice ran down the stairs with her letter to Edward, out
into a cold pink hood of light, across a flying grey
afternoon road towards the letter box, and back into her
room, where she scooped up a long piece of dark red silk
and walked about with it, finally draping it over the iron
bed-head. The silk trailed magnificently on to the
floorboards. It made her heart feel strong. She decided to
assemble her tools—for John Motton, so that John Motton
could properly know the nature of her profession—and she
began to line them all up on her table: her bone button
hook, her steel crochet hook, her porcelain thimbles, her
steel pinking shears, her needles in twenty-five sizes, most
probably one thousand pins, her measures and her wooden
blocks. In the late afternoon light each item beat out—a
small manifestation of human effort, of human discovery.
Now she gathered up all her fabrics and materials and laid
them out, on the floor and on the bed: the red silk, coarse
linen, navy blue velvet, all her cottons, net, lace, wools and
felts, taffeta, raffia, willow, wire mesh, hemp, flax, rubber,
steel wire; then the glues and lacquers, her starch and the
dyes. She announced to the image of John Motton on the
brown paper that all these things had been discovered
somewhere in the world. The indigo, for example, was
made from a leaf that grew in Bengal. Here were things that
had been brought here across continents, on horses and
mules; things that had lain in sacks, been hauled by men

from ship to factory, to be cut and dyed and pressed and steamed.

And here in her workroom, Alice made decisions about what to use when, in which combination, based on years of looking and touching and gauging, years of watching Mother design, measure, shape and stitch. Poor Mother. Those later years, with her fingers wretched with cold, desperate for their old strength and quickness. Alice rubbed her own hands together, thinking how she had held her mother's hands, their loose skin moving, trying to take all those years of her mother's work into her own fingers. She clenched her fist now, felt the hard muscle at the base of her thumb. Yes, Mother, see that strength. And then working for Madame in those narrow rooms: copying designs, weaving and coiling, studying anatomy, and philosophy, and *French*. Yes, Alice Heapy, Milliner—she had—Mr. John Motton, Sir—she too had *Knowledge*.

She had knowledge about these material things, but what she needed to know, surely, if she were to conquer her desire for John Motton (for what use was it? she could not marry the man; she would not wish to be his mistress; she did not know if she even liked him)—what she needed was his knowledge, to know about Human Nature. For what she realised was that she recognised only the physical parts of each person: their eyes, and their mouths, or their hands or the way they walked. If she saw light fall on their hair, she would be swept up into its rays. She could experience no one completely whole; for at any given moment, they were only a colour or a voice or a smell. And so she could not judge, she could not relate their features or their shape to a character trait or their morality. If she could judge, would she have suspected Joseph—? She stroked the cover of her blue book: was this where she would find the answers to her questions? For here lay Human Nature, described under the headings of forty-one seemingly random words, some of which simply made one laugh out loud: *Bibativeness*, for example, 'a fondness for liquids'. Or *Mirthfulness* itself: what if one had it in the seventh degree together with a minute portion of *Veneration*? Might such a one fail to benefit in any way at all from a gentleman's serious and scientific examination of one's skull? Indeed, it seemed to Alice that the whole point of the skull was not just physical protection for the brain, but protection from the acquisitive, prying eyes of men like John Motton.

The next afternoon Alice was cutting the fabric for Miss Thirsk's bashlik when Mrs. Peake brought up Edward's reply. He said, in his small, pencilled script:

'My dear sister,

It is a coincidence that you should write today: I have just this minute finished reading the Fowler book you mention—you may be surprised to learn that my wife purchased a copy of it only a few days ago. Father's book was George Combe's Constitution of Man, *I've got it here. It's more philosophical, more concerned with social reform, than this present version. I have heard it said that everybody had a copy of it in those days—it was almost as popular as the Bible! Of course, some of Combe's ideas have been discredited since—and Fowler's book doesn't purport to be much more than a guide to elf-improvement.*

Anyway, dear sister, the further coincidence is that Mr. Lorenzo Fowler himself is giving a public lecture tomorrow night, at his Institute in Ludgate Circus. Cassandra and I could meet you at The Civet Cat at six o'clock, as you suggested, and we can go all together to the Lecture at seven.

With affection,
your brother Edward.'

*

Alice was intrigued. She realised now that since Motton was working from the original principles of George Combe, and since Lorenzo Fowler was becoming very popular in London, he, John Motton, must be feeling a little bit piqued. Alice couldn't help smiling. She would certainly attend the Lecture. But first she would have to finish the wedding hood for Miss Thirsk, which would mean working all through the night again, for tomorrow morning she must also visit Mrs. Zaphinov. But now that she had ham, and bread, and coal, all was possible. In a minute, she would walk out and buy two ripe pears.

Alice decided to defy Phrenology by trying to love Mrs. Zaphinov as well as Mrs. Motton, to love even her arrogance and insensitivity. She would mentally embrace Mrs. Zaphinov's great curtain-skinned body and think kind thoughts. Yes, Alice thought as she darted through the streets towards Holland Park, let Mrs. Zaphinov's faults become her delights: let her arrogance be great, her insensitivity acute. Let her soak magnificently into the space left unoccupied by the perfectionist and the puritanical.

Mrs. Zaphinov stood opposite Alice in the frothy parlour. No, she *spilled* into the frothy parlour. She was lemony chiffon drifting amongst the *chaise longues* and tables. Despite her mission, Alice longed to say, *Sweep yourself up, madam, tuck yourself in.* She could just make out an expression on the woman's face: her great orange lips had parted and the lower one hung down to the left. She plumped down into a plump chair, her hands splayed on her knees, her bosom plunging and surfacing.

'Well then, my little milliner,' said Mrs. Zaphinov, 'I want *choux*, I want a hat with lacey *choux*, piled up like large profiteroles on a glassy plate.' She was rising half out of her chair, bolstered by desire.

'I know just the lace you would like, Mrs. Zaphinov,' Alice said. 'I bought a length in Whiteley's only last week. Here—they also have it in a very pale pink, and I could probably get your special apricot somewhere. Perhaps, something with a little silver and gold thread running through...'

Mrs. Zaphinov was swelling up, her chins were expanding with pleasure. She clapped her plump hands.

'Next Tuesday, Miss Heapy, no later! It is too perfect, I cannot be asked to suffer any delay in its realisation.'

And soon Alice was running up Silver Street to acquire lacy apricot choux, up into Notting Hill, on to the Grove and into Whiteley's, where the lace and ribbons were hung gaudy as Christmas streamers across the ceiling, brocaded ribbons, striped silk—every width, every texture of ribbon floats and streamers and tickles. She stood at the long counter in a crush of young women and their mothers, watching the girls unroll, stretch to a yard, roll, write out tickets and wrap up with paper. Every woman in London had streamers flying out behind them as they walked.

On the way back to her room, Alice began to think she should stay away from Phrenology and the Mottons, that she should surrender herself completely to the exacting work she must do for Mrs Zaphinov. Her only questions should concern how she could make the stitching invisible on lacy choux, on chiffon, or on the finest silk. She had the smallest needle and the finest thread; only if she kept up a quick, steady rhythm could she make the stitches small enough. She would have to work fast, to imagine her fingers were as tiny as a child's, small and smaller. She would shrink—it would be the work of a spider or a cricket. Yes, this is how she would work on the great voluptuous bonnet: with the pin-stickness of a spider or a cricket. It was for contrast: the larger the woman and the more outrageous the hat, then the more discreet, the more invisible, would be the milliner's work.

The hat could not be made of glass, the base of this hat —but Alice would make it *as if* it were glass: it would be a satin oval, pure oyster in colour, as glassy as she could make it by sewing it over with crystals and beads and tiny river pearls. It would catch the light like glass but it wouldn't be transparent, nor would it distort. On the satin base, the platter, Alice would build the coils of choux and chiffon into a lazy turban, much wider than Madame's head, a circumference of forty nine inches—and all to be placed on top of Madame's curly tresses by a series of ingenious clips and elastic and buttons. It would be utterly still, this gambling hat, yes, 'gambling', for Madame might as well go to the Casino in it—it was, thought Alice, surely a hat for acquisition and loss.

'Yes, next Tuesday, Mrs. Zaphinov,' whispered Alice to herself, 'next Tuesday I shall have something to show you.'
On Thursday evening Alice crept into The Civet Cat. Edward and Cassandra were sitting close together, sipping at glasses of beer when Alice arrived, and she had time to study them before they saw her. There they were, Edward, with his long pale sheep's face, and Cassandra, with her bright round red face: a slim umbrella, thought Alice, next to an open parasol. They sat close together, but it was as if Edward was sitting closer to Cassandra than she to him. Now he leapt up to embrace his sister. 'Here, have my beer, I'll get another one.'

'Are you sure this is a good idea, brother, us all going to a Phrenology lecture?'

Edward grinned his sheep's grin. 'Alice, the word that comes to mind is 'edification'.'

Cassandra said, 'Alice, Edward tells me you're making hats for a Phrenologist's mother. Fancy. It's very fashionable now, you know, having your head done.

Edward and I have been reading the book—I'd say by looking at you—let's see—*Secretiveness* and *Destructiveness*—both on the large side, and *Constructiveness*, of course, seeing as you're a milliner.'

'Oh Cassandra, ridiculous! How can you know any of these things? First of all, I'm wearing a hat. Second, your approach is too crude. Mr. John Motton told me himself that it is the "pattern of the relationship between the faculties" by which we can analyse…'

'Oooh, Mr. John Motton. Ooh Edward, apparently Mr. John Motton *says*…'

This is what Cassandra always succeeded in doing to Alice. She was clever and hurtful and she knew always how to trip Alice up. And this was just the beginning of the evening.

Cassandra insisted they travel on the new Metropolitan Railway to the Institute, though they could easily walk and save the fare. Edward shuffled behind Cassandra as she swept along, looking out of the corner of his eye towards Alice, hoping that Alice wouldn't make a fuss about his wife making a fuss. But in fact Alice was simply anticipating, thinking ahead about the American Fowler, an etching of whom graced the frontispiece of her little blue book: hair swept back from a lined forehead, long face, curly beard.

In the Hall, Edward sat respectfully; Cassandra took up a lot of room fanning her face with her gloves, and Alice noticed there were more women than men here, each with their chins jutting out of their coats at the exact same angle.

Fowler stepped wirily on to the stage and placed papers on the lectern. In a snappy drawl, if such is possible, he explained the basic principles of phrenological analysis, and soon a volunteer for delineation was procured from the audience, a young woman who could easily have been Alice herself: probably a seamstress or a governess, the earnestness drawing her face to a point. Fowler sat the woman down on a swivelling chair so that he could turn her, this way and that, first demonstrating her profile, then explaining the relationship of her crown to the frontal lobes. The young woman looked translucent. It was, thought Alice, as if she was thinning herself down with a solution in order that the Master's knowledge might enter her and replace whatever she previously knew about herself. Alice looked around the Hall at the people sitting forward on their chairs, their lips parted in agitation. At the end they clapped; Cassandra clapped loudly and stood up, and then Joseph was walking towards them, putting his arms around both Alice and Cassandra, drawing them into his chest, kissing them each on the cheek.

VIII

Alice decided that she would not tell John Motton that she had been to the Fowler lecture. Instead, she would study her blue book against the red book, the *Constitution of Man* that Edward had handed over to her at the Lecture. All this, when she hadn't yet delivered Miss Thirsk's hoods and burnouses, when Mrs. Zaphinov had yet to be crowned in her glass and lacy choux, and Mrs. Motton was clamouring for a new hat with gauze ruffles. Now, as Mary followed Alice towards the parlour, John Motton stepped out of his Consulting Room. 'Mother will be down in a moment, Miss Heapy,' and he led Alice by the arm into the familiar parlour and directed her towards a seat near the fireplace. She put her hatboxes on the table and sat down.

'I have a few designs I could be working on whilst I wait, Sir, I shall be perfectly—' but Motton was already lowering himself into a seat directly opposite her, his knees almost touching her own, and, as was his way, proceeded to stare, but this time did not speak. To distract herself from an energy that seemed to come from his knees, Alice asked him if he had heard the big gas explosion at Nine Elms last week.

'"*One vast upheaving of flame*" the newspapers called it,' she began. 'They say people up to a mile away were knocked to the ground.'

'It is the cost of progress, my dear. Gas has been created; gas will enlighten us,' he said. Alice wasn't sure if she should laugh.

She continued, 'My landlady, Mrs. Peake, says that she not only heard the explosion but dreamt the night before that it would happen. She believes she is clairvoyant.'

Motton raised his eyebrows, but his mouth did not move. Alice thought of something that would make his mouth move.

'Do you consider, Sir,' she held her breath, 'do you consider that she has large—*Sublimity*, or is it to do with the faculty of *Spirituality*?'

Motton exhaled. He stood up abruptly and walked over to the window, moving the lace curtains aside and peering out. Then he turned round—

'Heavens above, Miss Heapy. I can barely conceal my mirth. You—you help yourself to a little knowledge and think you have the truth of the very Universe. You read one line in an Encyclopaedia at the Municipal Library and think you can take the place of the Royal Astronomer.'

Alice stared up at him. He moved over to the fireplace, leaning against the mantelpiece. 'Listen, my dear Alice, it is all to do with *measurement*. Phrenology is the practical utilisation of knowledge based on scientific measurement; indeed, true knowledge can only be scientific. I am in the business of measuring and analysing both anatomy and what we call 'mind'. Now, it is necessary to examine the *quality* of the sections as well as their size, *in relation to each other*, as I have said before. We cannot simply deduce the precise formation of an individual's mind and character— here, your Mrs. Peake's mind and character—from her perceived ability to see into the future.

'You see, Alice, my profession is the result of the long and careful study of biology, philosophy and theology. It represents the pinnacle of our modern understanding of human nature.'

'But what about Charles Darwin?' Alice blurted out. 'Doesn't *his* work "represent the pinnacle of our modern understanding of human nature", Sir?'

'My dear Alice.' Motton paused.

Alice knew, in fact, very little about Charles Darwin, only what her father used to read to her from his copy of *Journal of Researches*, and once she was inspired by Darwin's description to draw a picture of a giant Galapagos tortoise with a bird on its head. She had not actually read any of his new book on the origin of the species.

'My dear Alice.'

Alice waited. John Motton's mouth was open now, the start of a smile perhaps, as if he found it really rather amusing, if a little tiresome, to have to engage with a young milliner on the immense subjects of understanding, human nature and science. In the silence Alice had time for regret. She fidgeted with her hatboxes, and cleared her throat, and it was this that seemed to set John Motton going once more.

'I have told you before, I am certain that Phrenology isn't simply a leisure pursuit for the acquaintances of my dear mother. I believe the work of Darwin supports our progressive project of making the world both rational and moral; indeed, he provides a useful model for our understanding of the hierarchy of intellectual and moral faculties over the lower animalistic organs.'

He stood up and again went over to the window, brushing against Alice's legs as he did so. 'Excuse me, Madam,' he said, and continued, 'Alice, I believe that men *and women* may determine their own actions. At any point in their lives they can begin to act in a rational manner that will be based upon the desire to enhance or diminish those faculties which undermine the harmony of their minds.'

These were noble ideas, thought Alice, but—proposed by a man who allowed himself frequent and close proximity to a young tradeswoman, who had a collection of miniature ivory ladies' legs and—this was almost worse—who had such a lazy way of moving his limbs.

'Perhaps you can best understand Phrenology's value, Alice, by considering its success in aiding men and women in their choice of marriage partner. Combe, for example, found a natural sympathy with a mature woman, and on examination of her faculties, he found that her *Benevolence, Conscientiousness, Firmness, Self-Esteem* and *Love of Approbation* were all well-developed. His was a most happy union.'

'But did he love her, Sir?'

'Did he *love* her?' Motton laughed, and Alice was aware of him looking at her shoulders. She began to get up, and his eyes moved up to her face, and at that moment Mrs. Motton entered the room. 'Ah, Mother—at last!'

And as Alice began to unwrap her magazines and drawings, she considered the conversation. John Motton had said to her that there was no knowledge that is not scientific. No knowledge, then, that had not been verified by human testing, no knowledge that was not the subject of repeated observations, no knowledge without application to general principles. Yet Alice had knowledge, she was sure. Knowledge that could not be proven and yet could not be called by any other name. Wasn't millinery the highest order of work, an elevated combination of science and art? All of her work proceeded according to physical laws: laws about proportion, colour, the strength and durability of threads, and balance. Whereas John Motton's work, she had begun to surmise, was rather—well, rather *speculative*. If it was accuracy and verification that Motton wanted, why, surely her hats could not be false, they could not be disproved. They had been hewn and wrought by her fingers, using her eyes, her memory, her imagination, and some inborn proclivity, some fierce propensity. And what was it for, John Motton's wish for accuracy and verification?

Alice made herself a promise. The next hat she made—for no-one in particular—would rise up from the head, like candy-floss in texture and as if a kindly breeze had caught it underneath. Above the raspberry floss there would be a hundred feathers on wire stems, as if scattered from above. It would be a hat for a moment of randomness.

Then, as Alice was discussing the designs with Mrs. Motton her eye alighted on an oil portrait of John Motton. She had not seen it before, and complimented Mrs Motton on its likeness.

'My dear, have a closer look. It is my husband—Johnny is his father's double,' said Belinda Motton. And indeed, the two men were almost indistinguishable, although Alice was truly shocked by her mistake. 'Now come upstairs, my dear. I want to show you something else.'

Alice followed Mrs. Motton up the wide staircase and into a bedroom: a big oak bed, cabinets, panelled doors. 'Come and see what kind of gentleman my husband was, Miss Heapy?' Mrs. Motton proceeded to fling open all the wardrobes, releasing a singeing wave of camphor. 'Look at this finery—don't you think he must have been a very fine man indeed?'

Alice began to move her right hand over the coats and jackets; she peered at the lapels and the seams, she rubbed cuff buttons between her fingers and thumbs. She could see at once how tall and broad Mrs. Motton's husband had been, how particular and methodical, and like his son, conservative in taste. Indeed, thought Alice, this surely was the wardrobe of the younger John Motton. She turned away from the jackets and tailcoats. Mrs. Motton was reflected in the mirror of the dressing table, awkward inside another dull olive costume. She was staring at Alice with her bird eyes, and Alice knew that Mrs. Motton loved that son of hers, her Johnny John, and that she suspected that Alice did also. What was true was that Alice would rather kiss John Motton than have him pronounce on her moral character. She had calculated that with a kiss they would be

69

equal, because during the kiss she could determine precisely whether the gossamer wet on the inside of John Motton's lips was of the *third* or *the fourth degree*, and then think about just what that was supposed to represent. Of course, it represented nothing at all and that was the joy of it. But if she agreed to a delineation—she would be laid out in discrete parts and sections and it might not be possible to put her back together again—or she might be put back wrongly. Perhaps that was the whole purpose: yes, thought Alice, put me back wrongly, Sir, for the greater good.

'He was very *particular*, Miss Heapy,' Mrs. Motton announced, pointing to what appeared to be a draper's chest, its glass fronts displaying the contents of each drawer. Cravats, in every shade of yellow, were laid in the drawers just as they would be in a draper's shop. Alice had a vision of the man draped all over with squares of yellow. Mrs. Motton opened one of the drawers, pulled out a cluster of the cravats and threw them down on the bed. The silk cravats: citron, mustard, turmeric.

'Fifteen years I have been a widow, Miss Heapy. Fifteen years.' Mrs. Motton seized a handful of the cravats, clutching them to her chest. 'And look at all these, Miss Heapy.' Mrs. Motton threw open another drawer and pulled out half a dozen white shirt collars. Then she suddenly sat down on the bed, putting her face in her hands: she was a forlorn green triangle amongst the white collars and the mustard silks and Alice at once knelt down opposite her, taking her hand in her own. 'Let me tell you, dear.' Mrs. Motton's voice was faint. 'Let me tell you.' She withdrew her hand from Alice's.

'Johnny was twenty years old when it happened. They were talking, father and son, they were talking rather loudly, Miss Heapy, they were arguing and they went out on to the street, both of them shouting. It was raining, I remember it was raining—pouring with rain. They were both angry, very

70

angry, and my husband must have fallen into—I wasn't there, I didn't see what happened.' Mrs. Motton took up one of the white collars and slowly unfurled it. 'Of course, they wouldn't let me look. I never saw him. Mary was there, she was terribly young then, but she held me, she kept me away, and I didn't see him there on the—road. I heard the driver screaming, he was hardly more than a boy himself. Johnny was kneeling down over his father, he was kneeling down in the road in his shirtsleeves, in the rain. He must have stepped off the pavement, I don't know. They were— Look dear, over there, at the daguerreotype, that's Johnny. Look, over there.' Alice looked. 'Poor boy, the driver I mean—I believe he never drove again afterwards. Of course, Johnny has all his father's books and papers. After the—after the accident he studied as hard as he could, with the best scholars and doctors, gentlemen who had been acquainted with my husband. And now, of course, now he has a *very* prestigious clientele of his own.' She put the collar down on the bed and took up one of the cravats. Alice saw that each cravat had a label, and that the labels bore the date, place of purchase, and the price.

'He is a loyal son, Miss Heapy, and it seems, a bachelor by nature. Yes,' she said, standing up and glancing towards Alice, 'a bachelor.'

Alice followed Mrs. Motton downstairs to look again at the drawings. The two women studied them in silence, except for the noise of Alice's heart beating in her ears. Then as Alice stood back to gain perspective, she knocked over a box of pins, and Mary was called in to help her pick them up. There they were, Mary and Alice on their knees, almost competitively claiming each pin whilst Mrs. Motton fussed around them, blocking the light.

In the morning, early, Alice waited in Hyde Park to see the military horses being exercised. The light was shining through the trees, lifting the dust from the track and suspending it in its rays. She was there for a purpose, to think about pageantry and to develop her ideas for Miss Thirsk's honeymoon hats; in particular to study the plumes that the horses have tucked in their forelocks—and it wasn't that she wished Miss Thirsk to have a plume sprouting from her forelocks, but she liked something about the angle at which the horses' heads were constrained by the harness, so that the plume moved almost independently and with greater majesty than if the horse were free of its straps. And when the horses plunged deeply through the dust, her heart would knock and she would imagine dying away amongst that galloping life force.

But there was so much to think about: John Motton and science and knowledge and knowledge of one's own nature, and artistry, and Joseph. And also John Motton and his father's death, and the yellow cravats, so carefully arranged in the draper's chest. For it seemed that Alice was destined to go back and back to the Mottons'. After the success of that first hat Mrs. Motton was becoming very demanding, encouraged, Alice suspected, by her son, the man who would have her cutting and blocking and stitching and steaming day and night whilst he thought of ever new ways of persuading her to submit to his analysis. Perhaps she was the only tradeswoman in the vicinity who remained virgin to the man's shiny callipers: no doubt he would have examined Mary very slowly and closely, and perhaps also the girl who collected and delivered the laundry, perhaps even the young boy Alice had noticed one day delivering John Motton's special tobacco. And why had Belinda Motton confided in her, or rather burdened Alice with this long-ago thing? What was she to do except feel yet more suspicious of the John Motton who she already could not erase from her mind? All right, she would be suspicious, as she had failed to be with Joseph; Joseph, who had squeezed her hand at the lecture, not in apology, but to see if he still had some place in her heart.

And then, on her way home, she noticed Madame D'Acier's windows were draped in black parramatta and crêpe and thick black muslin: mourning hats and veils, mourning caps, mourning capes. Lord Palmerston was dead. Within half an hour Alice was upstairs at Madame's, embroidering in gold thread, *Frangi, non flecti*, the Prime Minister's motto, inside the crowns of a row of mourning hats. She sat with a dozen young women and a couple of tiny girls, all stitching with tense, quick fingers. Everything suspended: every milliner and hatter and seamstress in the land would be black-blind for the death of Lord Palmerston. Black-blind and invisible, thought Alice; just what she needed to be. But it made her think of her mother, and how all through the mourning period Alice had noticed how her eye was drawn to colour, to the leaves of the almond trees, to a blue moth, to figs and apples and loganberries. And now, embroidering the letters, Alice remembered her dream, where Edward was looking up at her from the pool, like Mother used to from her bed, with the dark green satin all round her. She had been beautiful, like an angel, until her illness had caused her to sail forever on those dense satin waves, with the salt building up in the crevices and folds of her skin. But it was Edward who suffered most in those days. His dreams were full of termite mounds and volcanic islands, and if boys could have grown old men's beards at the age of fourteen, then Edward's beard would have been greyer and longer than any man's.

In the end neither she nor Edward could bear to look at Mother, the sea-witch, with her long white and auburn hair separating into serpents. They could not bear to look at her; Alice and Edward had taken down all the mirrors and wrapped them up in newspapers. Today Alice thought she should have studied her mother's ruined face; that she would have found the beauty still trapped there. Mother, slowly ossifying, and she, Alice, and Edward clinging to each other lest they also be sucked down beneath the seabed, sucked down to a place that permitted no reflection.

But Alice would make hats for Mother; every hat she would make would be a spectacle and a wonder; every hat and bonnet and cap, a miracle of ingenuity; every hat would bring beauty back to her Mother. *Frangi, non flecti: broken but not deflected.*

Alice was discussing more designs with Mrs. Motton the next day, distracted by her own contemplations on the differences between Fowler and Motton, when Mrs. Motton started to talk once again about the death of her husband under the wheels of the hansom.

'He should have seen me in my new hats,' she said, and began to weep. She stood up and sat down, looked at her face in the mirror, and wept a little more as Alice gathered up her drawings.

'Let me bring your son to you, Mrs. Motton,' Alice said, and as she walked towards the Consulting Room she could hear John Motton's voice, its aerated clips discharging what might be wisdom to an invisible patient. She listened for a response, and heard a woman's voice, a teasing giggle between each of Motton's phrases, the same voice she'd heard before. The door handle turned, and Alice dropped back down the hall, unbreathing, as the woman emerged from the Room. Motton followed her out and immediately noticed Alice, his mouth con torting in surprise and displeasure. He continued to show the woman out—she was magnificently red, brocadely black—and then turned to Alice—'Spying on me again, Miss Heapy?'

'Sir, excuse me, I was merely concerned for your mother. I think you should know that your mother seems very upset today and I wondered if perhaps you should call her physician.'

Motton ushered Alice into his Room. It smelt strongly of the woman: floral, milky. He shut the door and folded his arms. He did not suggest Alice sit down. She folded her own arms.

'A few days ago Mrs. Motton described to me how your father died.'

Motton stared past her towards the window.

'I'm sorry if this distresses you, Sir—'

'Whatever you have to tell me, Miss Heapy, I would ask that you simply get on with it.'

'She explained to me at my last visit how your poor father—the hansom, Sir...'

Motton began to flick noisily through some papers on his desk.

'As you may imagine, Miss Heapy,' he began without looking up, 'the event was indeed profoundly distressing. Such events produce agitation in the mind, even many years after the event. Take no heed, Madam—let my mother weep, and get on with your business here.'

'Forgive me, Sir.' She didn't want to go away from him yet; she was still breathing in the woman's scent. She decided to strike up again. 'I wanted to tell you also, Sir, that I attended a lecture recently, at the Institute at Ludgate Circus, a lecture given by Lorenzo Fowler, the American. I wondered, are you an admirer of his?'

Perhaps Alice should have asked whether or not Fowler was an admirer of John Motton. He stared at her without replying. Alice thought she could see a small smudge of lipstick at the side of his mouth.

'I disagreed with him on a particular point,' Alice persisted. Motton raised his eyebrows. 'He said, Sir, that sensations are cerebral, so that *all* is cerebral, as if there are no other phenomena in the world, so that everything we experience is, ultimately, dependent on the mind. I am certain this cannot be the case.'

That roused him.

'Miss Heapy, you are a milliner. How can you be *certain* that one of the main principles of Phrenology is incorrect?'

'Perhaps it is *because* I am a milliner, Sir.'

Motton swung round to Alice's side of the desk, gripped her upper arms and pulled her towards him. Alice's nose was almost touching his shoulder, she was aware of her stinging flesh. He released her and walked slowly back to his chair.

'Alice. Alice Heapy. The only way you will begin to understand my profession, and whether or not I agree with that modern populariser of Phrenology, Mister Lorenzo Fowler, is by allowing me the privilege of examining you. I shall not, of course, charge you for my services. Why don't we make an appointment for you now?' He was opening his Appointments Book. 'Let it be a day on which you do not have a fitting with my mother. I think you...'

But Alice didn't wish to hear what John Motton thought. 'Mr. Motton, I think we should attend to your mother now,' she said, and walked out of the Room leaving the door open. She collected her basket from the parlour, reassured Mrs. Motton that her son would be along in a moment, and left the house. In Motton's eyes, she realised, she had become a man-woman; it was as if he had seen whiskers sprouting from her cheeks, and he thought he could turn her, by this alchemy—by examining her—back into a woman.

That milliner, thought John Motton, is making *me* ill. I have only five minutes to re-calculate the measurements on the Lindsey boy so I can give his father, who will arrive early, a reasonable picture of the poor stupid lad, and here's Miss Alice Thruppenny-Heapy demanding that I listen to her prying questions on the pretext that my mother is unwell. She's like a crochet hook, poking and picking at me.

But Motton laid down his pen and went to find his mother. She was indeed looking a little faint, and he caught up her hand and knelt beside her. 'Mother, I shall call the physician directly.' He was still thinking about the Lindsey boy, who was fourteen years old, and as he knelt he thought of his own father, and how his father would take him into the Consulting Room when *he* was fourteen or fifteen to measure his chest and his arm-span. Writing down the measurements, making notes and comparisons, doing nothing to disguise the look of displeasure as he checked the figures a second, a third time. Checking the measurements again, trying to contain the measurements, as if they had their own life.

And yet there is attraction there, he thought; he was a little, how should he put it, a little *aerated* by Alice Heapy's presence.

IX

That afternoon Alice struggled to turn right into Campden Street, towards Miss Thirsk's house. The sky had darkened and a terrible wind sucked her lips away from her teeth. He'd been so agitated, John Motton, so impatient, bristling inside his ginger jacket. Bricks from a chimneystack glanced off a pillar-box and broke up on the road in front of her. She shouldn't have mentioned his father. She shouldn't have seen his—lady-friend.

Miss Thirsk pulled Alice off the step into the hallway and quickly shut the door.

The fire had gone out because of the wind, and the two women sat in the kitchen next to the range, where Miss Thirsk announced that she had given up attending poetry readings, that she was bored with poets who wanted a redeeming woman with hair to the waist. That she had joined, instead, the Women's Discussion Society, and would now turn her head towards tall women with muscular lips.

But soon she would leave for the west coast of Ireland, for her gentleman was an Anglo-Irish industrialist; he would care for her absolutely, she said, he would wrap her in cashmere, he would carry her over the muddy paths and place her before a peat fire in the county of Cork.

'I shall let him take me over the bogs and the hills in his arms, Miss Heapy, for he has the face of an innocent child and the bald pate of an elderly man. It is what I admire about him, the mixture of child and mature man.'

As she spoke Alice could hear an Irish lilt to Miss Thirsk's voice; she had already imbibed him, she was flushed with the difference a man makes, a difference Alice felt every time she thought of John Motton. She understood Miss Thirsk's delight, even though her gentleman was indeed rotund and red-faced and short, for he was yet a man—'And there is much to consider in any man,' said Alice.

'In particular by candlelight,' said Miss Thirsk, 'and as he sighs and snuffles, full of hope. Yet it's not for love, you know, Miss Heapy. It is for the sumptuous sensation of being admired. It is as if I am in a gilded cage of my own design, and my fiancé circles it and peers in at me. I am untouchable because I do not love him. Of course, he loves me, but purely in the manner of a voyeur. He knows he cannot touch me without burning his hand on the golden bars. They represent money, you know, for he has bought me with, and for, these golden bars. He can see only interrupted portions of me at any given time, never the whole, and that is the pleasure of it.'

Alice laughed, although she felt a chill creeping over her.

'You laugh, Miss Heapy, perhaps you have understood my little joke. You thought I was sad and serene, did you not? Indeed I was, until my gentleman came to me from the great gondola that moves slowly across land—and I am no longer sad, as I say, not because I am loved, nor because I love (which I do not) but because of the existence of my golden cage and my voyeur. It is a perfect match. It is perfection itself.

'Now Alice, I trust you will not give yourself away to some literal man, one who wants you to strip to the waist, who wants to roll your breasts up and down like a pastry-man. No, no, no, promise me, my sweet Miss Alice Heapy, that you will choose a man who will maintain his dignity in your presence, choose a man for whom you will represent the highest point of Grace, for whom Love is an ideal form, not an excuse to twitch and fondle—

'I say to my gentleman, "You may kiss me now" and I offer him my gloved hand through the bars of the cage, and the more lightly he brings his lips to my fingers, the more charmed I am. Should he wet my glove, my long glove that extends to the top of my arm, he should have to return to his gondola and glide on to a new landing post. I am delicate, you see Alice, I can barely be touched. Indeed, measure me no more, my dear—henceforth you will have to divine that which you wish to know of me.'

Miss Thirsk's neck was long, her brow high, her lip still malformed and beautiful. She believed in Love as an ideal form. That was all that Alice needed to know of Miss Thirsk. And she, Alice, would pledge never to engage with a literal man.

'But come to the next Women's Discussion meeting, Alice, do come. They talk about the *Phrenologists* there, about the *Craniologists*, who measure and find wanting.'

'Oh no, Miss Thirsk.' *Every person in London in the thrall of the Phrenologists.* 'I have so many designs and hats to complete…' *and anyway, I have no interest in such matters.*

'Come to *one* meeting. You will be surprised.'

'But I shall have to work through several days and nights, ma'am,' *with the darkness staring in at me, accusing and inviting, with infinity beckoning, when the hats were nearly done, when I had to finish by the morning, when Mother and Mrs. Buzzing Bee could have been dead by the morning, with goose feathers over their eyes.* 'I cannot.'

The two women stared past each other, thinking their separate thoughts, listening to the rattle of the windows and the rain, until—something struck the glass and slithered to the ground. Alice pressed herself up against the window. She could see blue amongst dark feathers and a thread of gold.

'It's a jay!' Alice needed that bird. She had said she would not use feathers, but Mrs. Motton had insisted. She must, Mrs. Motton had said, she must have a hat fashionably picturesque with feathers and shells and fruit.

'Oh, let me take it home, Miss Thirsk.'

Miss Thirsk looked at Alice with amused suspicion.

I shall place it in hot water until the feathers come away from the body. I shall weave its beautiful feathers into a headdress.

Neither woman spoke as Alice wrapped the bird in a piece of muslin from her workbasket. As Miss Thirsk showed her to the door Alice noticed a visiting card on the table in the hall. *Dr. Firbank, Phrenologist*—a Farringdon address. Alice looked at Miss Thirsk; she looked back at Alice, with her lips pressed into a small smile, and she picked up the card between her thumb and forefinger, twisting it close towards Alice's face.

'My aunt,' she said, 'my aunt recommends her Phrenologist to everyone she knows. She boasts that he makes the finest delineations in the land.'

Alice slipped the card into her pocket.

The wind pushed Alice back to Notting Hill. A large piece of zinc roofing blocked the terrace and a cart was lying on its side in the main street. Alice feared for her little muslin parcel and clutched it to her chest. Once at home she could barely shut the front door against the wind and Mrs. Peake was shrieking in the hallway. All the papers from the table flapped about the two women's heads and they had to put the full force of their bodies into closing the door. Mrs. Peake tried to detain Alice, fussing about the wet soot that had just a minute ago spattered her best front parlour, but Alice only cared about her dead bird, and crept upstairs to set about preparing her enamel basins and solutions.

There she rested, Alice's jay, on a white cloth on the table, greasy, her tawny head stiff and proud. The azure on her wing moved into lilac, purple, black, a little gold, like the scales on a fish, and there was more gold almost concealed beneath the downy dusky feathers. The con tour feathers were as fine as fine netting: mink, dun, a little bronze, ginger, and underneath, the insulation was as soft as fur against the taffeta of the bright patterned wing. Alice realised now that in fact she wanted the bird for Miss Thirsk rather than Mrs. Motton: for Miss Thirsk was azure moving into lilac, purple, black, with a little gold concealed beneath. She stroked the bird for Miss Thirsk. She must quickly sketch the pattern, get her paints out and try to replicate those colours. She held the bird in the palm of her free hand as she painted: it gave her a feeling of equilibrium, to hold this creature in her hand, working to immortalise it.

Last time the bird was a black redstart, very rare. She had blanched it in boiling water, and soon all the feathers were out, scattered around the bird, still protecting its forlorn, pink skin. Of course, she could not afford to be sentimental, and quickly gathered the feathers up, placed them in another bowl (regrettably her white washing bowl), stirred them gently round with a wooden spoon and laid them on a cloth. When she returned to the drowned bird, she wished that she also could be placed in a solution, let her own plumage be washed, removed, dried, sprayed and placed in boxes inside drawers.

But this bird—this one must remain perfect. First she must make a saline solution to preserve the skin and she would have to find a muscle for the injection, for which she would need the syringe and the arsenical powder for the mites. The beautiful, beautiful bird: it fit between Alice's two cupped hands, it was so light, five ounces, six perhaps. She cradled it, smoothing its gossamer-net feathers, tapping her nail against the hard beak: it glistened like wet bark, almost bronze in the stormy light. She lifted the bird to find the muscle between the wing and the torso.

All was assembled. Alice laid down the bird on its white cloth once again and turned it over. Its long back was proud and graceful even in death, especially in death. She knelt down and recited a small prayer: *O spare me a little, that*

I may recover my strength: before I go hence, and be no more seen.
Then she took the bird and made the incision. She cut
from the centre of the top of its breast to its tail; she peeled
back the skin as if it were her own, cut the tissue away from
the skin and lifted out the organs. They slipped coolly from
her bloodied fingers on to the white cloth. The smell made
her retch—fishy, gaseous—yet she continued, and cut
away, as delicately as she could, the brain and the eyes.
Now there were two birds. She cleaned the shell with damp
rags. She placed the wood wool inside the cavities, tucking
it up with her fingertips, watching the arsenical powder
freckle the red mass. She sewed the skin over the eye
sockets, and began to sing to the bird, to sing a child's
lullaby.

The bird weighed so little now. Alice spread its wings
and pinned them. She would paint the feet azure and the
legs gold, not for Mrs. Motton, no—but for the strange,
caged living of her beautiful Miss Thirsk.

Alice went out to Kensington High Street to buy some
apples. When she returned she found Mrs. Peake had
slipped a letter under the door; it was a letter from Edward.
She put her parcel down on her worktable and opened the
letter. Edward had again visited the Institute at Ludgate
Circus. He had, he said, enjoyed private discourse with Mr.
Lorenzo Fowler. *Private discourse.* And now he wished to
have the same with the—as he put it—'the only slightly less
eminent' John Motton. Would Alice please arrange an
introduction? *Would Alice arrange an introduction?* He
proposed to—*to train in the New Phrenology*—during the
evenings, and eventually to cease his work as a hat-blocker.
'I am, as you know, dear sister, pitifully short of money,
and Cassandra says I must try to seek remuneration from
every possible source.'

Alice put the letter down. How could it possibly help Edward to have the acquaintance of John Motton, who, after all, practiced what she presumed was the *old* Phrenology? She took up a knife and cut a slice of apple, trying to formulate her response to Edward's request. But poor Edward, how he must suffer with that round hard cheese of a wife. Finally she wrote:

'Dearest Edward,
Pronouncement and exhortation, Edward—that is the business of Phrenology! I cannot think that it will suit you. Please do not ask me to introduce you to John Motton. In any case, he would not like you to mention Mr. Fowler. I understand from my few discussions with Mr. Motton that there are some important and irreconcilable differences of principle between the New and the Old Phrenology.
    Your loving sister,
    Alice.'

The following afternoon Alice received another letter from Edward. He *must* see John Motton, Cassandra insisted upon it. He said he would be sure not to mention Mr. Fowler, and would flatter Mr. Motton at every opportunity.

The next morning, Alice's washbasin had ice in it. If ice did not melt she could have slipped it under her garments to keep her cool whilst she wrote the letter to Mr. John Motton, in which she must ask if she might introduce her brother into his venerable Consulting Rooms. But she did not need ice: she had a circle of silver satin that she could cut into shards. She wrote the letter.

    That very evening there was a light knocking at Alice's door. It was Mary. She said nothing, she did not ease herself into the room, she did not stare rudely; she simply handed Alice a plain white card which bore a short message: *Wednesday, at five o'clock.*

X

John Motton was enclosed in the winged armchair by an inexplicably dark fireplace. Mary directed Edward and Alice to a narrow embroidered settee, where they perched. They learnt that Mrs. Motton's physician had confined her to her bed for a fortnight. Alice thought Motton's eyes were a little further back in his head than usual; his shoulders seemed lower.

'Your sister has displayed a keen interest in Phrenology, Mr. Heapy—a family concern, clearly. I am sure she would make a fine Phrenologist herself, were the profession a suitable one for young women.'

'Ah yes,' Edward nodded his head and smiled with his mouth open. Alice could not tell whether or not Motton was teasing. Edward had told her women were already training at the Ludgate Institute. Edward began to talk very quickly:

'Sir, I have been studying the French Utopian Socialist, Charles Fourier, and I must reveal to you, Sir, that having begun so faithfully, so enthusiastically working on Gall and Spurzheim, I do in fact find Fourier's idea of a dominant *passion* holding the rudder of individual character offers a most compelling alternative to the principles of Phrenology. And I have come to you today, Sir, to see if you can restore my faith, as I cannot make a living from espousing the principles of a French Utopian Socialist whose ideas have no currency in London today. I must have an income you see, Sir, since machinery is replacing many of us at hat-blocking, and I cannot of course advertise as a Fourierian or as a Master of the Passions, Sir.'

Edward chuckled a little, the chuckle developing into a cough. This was not what Alice had expected. She was impressed at her brother's cunning. Motton straightened up a little but did not reply. Alice imagined him making his rapid assessment of her brother with his long low face and his prominent occipital regions. Edward talked quickly into the silence.

'But I would agree, Sir, that once one begins to study character and human nature itself, one is possessed by the most insatiable curiosity to know and understand one's own and everyone else's character, and...' Edward scrunched up his face, 'and their lives, their moral propensities.'

Motton reached for and opened his snuffbox.

'As to the matter of classification, Sir, ah the pleasure to be had in creating pattern and hierarchy. And the idea of self-knowledge as the foundation stone of self-improvement—ah, truly intoxicating, I agree, I agree, but Fourier's *Passions*, Sir...'

Motton did not look at Edward but Alice could see that he was preparing his answers from that special pre-selection he kept in his dense lobes. Or perhaps he would find the answers in the snuffbox itself. To Alice's dismay, Edward continued with his astonishing monologue.

'And Sir, what else should we do with our lives? Is it not our higher purpose to examine and analyse, to situate the anomalous within a pattern, to study the logic of contradiction? Is that not our—almost *Divine*—mission, Sir? Ah, how I respect your work, Sir, and of course your father's work. When Alice said she was Milliner to your dear mother, forgive me, Sir, forgive me, I felt proud, yes, proud. And yet if I may pursue my train of thought for a moment, on the subject of Charles Fourier...'

Alice pressed her leg against Edward's. He certainly didn't need to persuade John Motton of the benefits of a different system to that on which the man's eminence was built. Alice looked intently towards her brother, she breathed towards him, but he did not notice. He wilfully did not notice. Then Mary knocked at the door, bringing in the tea tray, setting it down amongst the three, and Motton finally interrupted Edward—

'Yes, very interesting, Mr. Heapy. I must admit that I have not studied Monsieur Fourier—I have found there is quite enough to learn about Phrenology without being distracted by competing theories of character. And I find the principles upon which Phrenology is built to more than adequately help us to explain what we need to know about character and mind. I might counsel you to devote yourself rather longer to the scientists Gall and Spurzheim—and Combe, of course—before you allow your mind to be manipulated by the persuasive and, let us say, *incontinent*, Utopians.

'Of course, what the Utopians are unable to do, by their nature, is to render the intangible tangible. Far from being able to predict human behaviour from minute and repeated observations, you must agree, young Sir, the Utopians simply *invent* human behaviour to suit their beliefs.'

Edward opened his mouth; Motton continued,

'Phrenology is, by contrast, a *material* philosophy of life. As Combe has said, the original constitution of man *is* perfection. As you will know, and as I was explaining to your sister only recently, each of the known Faculties within the human mind has a normal action; that normal action fulfilled is perfection; any abnormal action is imperfection. Each of the Faculties should therefore be cultivated by supplying each with its proper aliment. All the Faculties must be brought into harmonious concert with each other so that each of us, and the whole of society, may live perfect lives. Your sister understands this, Mr. Heapy.'

'Forgive me, Sir,' cried Edward, 'but that is surely just as Utopian, just as ideal a philosophy as anything the socialists have espoused. *The beau ideal.*' Edward laughed a funny little laugh. '*Harmonious concert.* It is just like Fourier—it is musical, you know, Sir—the Master assigns to each of us a note or a place in the musical scale. Isn't that charming, Alice, Mr. Motton? You see Sir, every Dominant has a variety of shades that must be discriminated and named and we have a gamut of Tonics, each shade being the Tonic passion. You see it is from an entirely different sensibility that Fourier operates, a French rather than a German sensibility—thus we have '*Les Passions*' and there is, apparently, no equivalent word in German, and of course the English word does not match it in any way. Nevertheless, the Master insists that the passion that must be called the Dominant passion holds the rudder of a character. For example, the Dominant of the miser is his ambition, of which avarice is a sub-shade or even a development...'

Of course! That was the sound Alice heard when the air wisped through John Motton's front teeth: it was ambition, the desire for status—it was aspiration aspiring him. By contrast, each hat she made seemed to represent a complete journey. She must start again each time: each of her ladies, in each season. She could not even think 'last year the cerise suited Madam, therefore I shall make another just like it', for this year it would not suit her. Each hour, each day and night of sewing and shaping was complete; each stitch was absolute.

Edward was still speaking. 'Of course, Fourier is in fact wholly *opposed* to the idea of Character *per se*. Ah, the Phrenologists, if only they could read a little French. Then there are the *Polymixts*, ambiguous 'characters' who have *Ralliant*—that's two passions—that hold the rudder; and numbers and notes. It is so delightfully architectural, it makes Phrenology look like—No, no, no—here we have mathematics, so that there are twelve orders: that is to say, five *Senses*, four *Affectives*—that is to say, friendship, love, familism and ambition—and three *Distributives*: love of intrigue, love of variety and cumulation of pleasures…'

Alice put her hand on her brother's arm. 'Let us drink our tea,' she said, looking at him earnestly. This was what Edward was like: he offered himself up, wholly unguarded; he offered up the sum of his existence to the moment, he laid out before him all that rendered him Edward Heapy. He knew nothing of holding back part of himself, he knew nothing of concealment; for he had plans for justice—and she should never have agreed to bring him here, to put him at the mercy of John Motton, because Edward was laying out his plans before a man who, Alice had decided—despite, or was it because of—his profession, had no place in his heart for simple justice. Justice! Alice believed John Motton would not recognize the concept. 'Justice, Mr. Heapy?' she could imagine him saying, and Motton would only be able to repeat the word: *Justice*. It would remain inert on his lips. He would try again. He would barely shape his lips to make the correct sound and the word would stay in the cavity of his upper palate. And yet opposite John Motton, the tall and broad, confidently-whiskered Motton—Edward looked slight and hunched, he looked yet more diminutive.

John Motton was rising to his feet, he was placing his tea cup on the mantelpiece next to a gold-lipped china dog. Edward's eyes were turned upwards, taking in the room, the portraits, the dark moss, the dark blue glass and the burgundy. Then Mary appeared at the door again, this time holding a plate of cakes. Motton beckoned to her and she put the cakes down on the table. She looked at Edward, she sucked Edward into her orbit. Mary had secrets, she was a carrier, she was a harbour. Alice felt a bead of sweat on her lip.

Motton looked down at poor Edward; he judged him—it was a palpable thing. It was as if John Motton allowed his physical superiority to take the place of moral superiority. But the two men could not be compared. Alice's brother Edward could not, must not, be compared with John Motton.

The room was so warm. Edward was standing up now. He was agitated, he was loosening his neck tie and pulling open his jacket. Alice remembered when Edward was about ten or eleven years old, he brought Mother violets in a tiny blue vase, finding her tipped sideways with pale vomit on her pillow. He placed the violets on the bedside table and held her hand. 'The violets,' he had said to Alice afterwards, 'I thought I could make Mother better with the violets.' What would Phrenology say about that, offering the skull as the only arbiter of all propensities? *Crack open Edward's skull, Mr. Motton! Crack open mine! Don't bother with the reassembly.*

Mary was already collecting up plates, taking the untouched cakes away, taking the half-full china tea cups away. 'Shall I light the fire now, Sir?' she asked. There was an intimacy between them, complicity. Alice could see it on Mary's white face with its dark mole: the entrance to the darkness of her master's secrets.

'Yes, Mary, light the fire.'

'But it is already too warm,' Edward protested.

'You may leave, Sir, if you experience discomfort.'

Why did Edward stay, thought Alice, why did they stay?

'I experience discomfort, Sir, and yet I wish to stay. I believe we have not finished our business, Sir.'

'We have no business, Sir; you are simply taking up my time.'

'We have business, Sir.'

Indeed, there had been, so far, no exchange of information; only Edward espousing an alternative theory of character, upon which Motton had barely remarked. Mary had been hesitating, looking from one man to the other, her face inscrutable. Now she took a taper and lit the fire. It was six in the evening; the fire must be lit. It spat, and hissed.

'Let me begin again, Sir,' persisted Edward. 'What I am most interested in, Sir, is how we *as a class* might benefit from the application of Phrenology. Let me talk to you of the body politic, of the way it may be divisible in the same way as the human mind: divisible into the *propensities, the sentiments, the perceptions, and the reflective*. Let me talk to you about how we might apply the Phrenological categories to a whole society...'

John Motton stood firm at the edge of the fireplace. His eyes burned the sister and the brother. 'Phrenology,' he growled, 'has, in the past, precipitated much social reform, in the mental asylums and in our prisons—but it does not offer an analysis of character that encourages a socialist system. As you well know, Robert Owen's experiment failed. You cannot apply Phrenology to the body politic in so crude a fashion. Society requires the correct knowledge of and utilisation of men's propensities in the service of Industry and Science. Indeed, we are in the grip of a scientific revolution. The artisan class itself, for example: we do not need it as we once did, and even less do we need hat blockers imagining they can turn themselves into Phrenologists within ten days.'

'Sir,' Edward rose up, 'I do not wish to offend your hospitality, but I simply cannot remain seated whilst you cast aspersions on the artisan class. I cannot but defend the group to whom my allegiance is pledged. Sir, surely you know that it is an historic moment for artisans in this country, today? Do you not recognize the great need to preserve our traditions and skills, and how it is ever more important to teach our young men and women...'

John Motton was standing taller and yet broader. His large dark head was reflected in the mirror over the mantelpiece. Edward was speaking bravely but he was trembling, he was a fish, a sacrificial lamb.

Alice whispered, 'Edward, do not take it to heart. I am sure he is not serious,' although she knew little wit in the John Motton of her acquaintance. She suddenly wished for all humour, all mirth, to take this scene over, to take her over. She even rubbed the sides of her head where Wit was supposedly located.

'I am serious, Madam.'

Alice's heart beat outside her dress. She took Edward's elbow and eased him towards the door, eased him out into the hall. Poor sensitive foolish blind Edward, lashed permanently to his dreams. They edged down the corridor, Mary sliding ahead of them, opening the front door; they were on the steps, down the steps, gone from the rage in John Motton's eyes.

Edward and Alice looked red-faced at each other on the pavement. Alice gripped Edward's forearm and pulled him towards The Civet Cat. Inside they scored their throats with gin. Alice said she would not forgive him. She told him he looked like a sheep, a pasty, silly sheep and she could share, at that moment, Cassandra's frustration, even wonder at her powers of endurance.

'How could you, Edward? How could you?'

Edward stared straight ahead, cradling his glass, his lips forming a messy, foolish smile. He said, in a voice as similar to Motton's as he could get: 'There is no such thing as Edward Heapy, hat block-maker. Denied his function, Edward Heapy has ceased to function.'

'You were trying to get the better of him, Edward. You should have known he would retaliate.'

'I *did* get the better of him, though I swear that was not my original intention.'

'What *was* your original intention, Edward?'

'For goodness sake, Alice, you know I just did it for Cassandra. It's all for Cassandra, who wants to rise up, who wants to be *bourgeois*. I was content to work in the blockers by day and study the Utopians at night—and on a Sunday afternoon if I was lucky.' He groaned, then he was up. 'Let's get another gin.'

'No,' said Alice.

'Then listen, dear sister, listen. In a minute I shall go home to my rooms. I shall recognise my rooms by Cassandra's lacy curtains at the windows. I shall be clumsy with the gin. I shall sit down at my kitchen table and tap my knee. Then I shall lay my head down on my arms. After a while I shall creep into my bedroom and lay down beside my sleeping wife. And I shall whisper, *'You see, Cassandra, my sweet pet, it is all about Mathematics, and Love, dear Cassandra. Mathematics and Love! Ah my sweet, are you really asleep, my dear Cassandra, dear wife? Let me look at you then, let me kiss your pretty cheek.'* And I shall say, for my wife needs to know these things, *'Do you know, Cassandra, what I said to Mr. John Motton? I said: tell me, Sir, what you consider to be the role of artisans in this country, today, at this historic moment? Did he not know, I asked, of the great need to preserve our traditions and skills, ever more important to teach our young men and women—ah, Cassandra dear, you are so pretty in your sleep – and he replied, he said to me, he had the gall to say—Gall!—do you like that?—he had the very gall to say to me, my dear, that there is no such thing as the artisan class. That we have ceased to function. No longer have a function. It is progress, he said, we were in the grip of progress. If I were not an atheist, I would say now, Let us pray, dear wife, Let us pray!'* And at this point I shall ask her, *'Let me touch you a little, my dear, let me warm you. Let me warm you a little, my darling, darling wife.'*

'Stop it, Edward,' cried Alice.

He continued, *'Cassandra. Cass-an-dra—your special name, my special love. You are but the perfection of human nature my*

93

dear—is it not that to which we all aspire? But it will not come about on account of Phrenology, little wife. So let Fourier's 'Passions' be taken up instead, my dear. And let me warm you a little, my dear. Here, and here, ah, come on, a little kiss, please, at last, Cassandra, surely one little kiss?' And she will remain asleep, Alice, she will remain in the deepest sleep.'

'Come, Edward, that is enough. I shall leave you here,' said Alice, and left the pub without him.

Two days later Alice received a letter from Mr. John Motton. He wrote that his mother had taken a turn for the worse. He enclosed one guinea for the most recent hat designs and asked Alice to cease work on them as he feared his mother might not survive the winter.

Alice looked at the platter hat she had been constructing for Mrs. Motton. Covering the base was a mound of tiny silk leaves, their veins embroidered almost imperceptibly with silver thread; the second, unfinished, layer consisted of blue-gold feathers and sugared almonds and mother of pearl. Alice laid the money out on her work table. It was less than she was owed. If only Edward hadn't—if only Cassandra hadn't—if only she, Alice, would just cease to work on anything other than her millinery. If only she were not a little in love with a Phrenologist, a man she didn't even like, a man who had no respect for hard-working artisans.

She went outside into the rain. The lamps were already lit at four o'clock. She would get muddy and cold, she would let the season do its work on her. She could smell the sweat of damp horses, the tarpaulin on the barrows, wet newspaper; she listened to the noise of wetness, wheels on gravel, hooves echoing in the dark grey rain. She let her fingers get cold and red. She had no umbrella and her uncoiled hair lay cool over her neck. She walked up and down the High Street, she turned into Bird Walk and leant against the wall of the church; and then she was in Church Street, it was dusk, and she was only yards from the Mottons' house. There was a carriage waiting outside, the driver and the horse were hunched against the rain. Perhaps it was the physician? Alice waited. It was five o'clock, half past that hour. A tall fellow emerged, with a doctor's case. Alice strained to catch the expression on his face. She could barely see. The carriage drove away. It was six o'clock, her cheeks burned with the cold, and now Motton appeared. He descended the steps quickly, put up his umbrella, and walked with great strides towards Notting Hill. Alice followed him; she followed him in the rain, up Silver Street into the Grove, into Holland Park Road, all the way to Holland Park Mansions where he slipped through a side door. Through the patterned glass of a tall window she could see him climbing up stairs.

She waited in a doorway, opposite Holland Park Mansions, in the rain.

John Motton's mistress does not greet him. She faces away from him in the glow of candlelight; he must stand at the edge of the room. She is dressed only to the waist. She crouches over a porcelain bowl and begins to wash herself. He watches as she takes the soap and lathers her hands, he watches as she slides her lathered hands between her thighs, as she rinses and pats herself dry with a towel. He moves towards her, moves round to face her. She holds the towel across both her hands. He takes the towel slowly from her, bringing his eyes up to meet hers. He presses the towel over his mouth. She watches him. He places the towel on a chair and moves back to the edge of the room. She turns towards him. She unlaces her corset and from the other side of the room he can see her beautiful dark textured nipples. She lies down on her *chaise longue*, with her corset open; she moves her legs a little apart. She remains absolutely still, like an artist's model. He stands at the edge of the room, his hands aching to feel her skin. He cannot touch her. They do not speak. He cannot reach her; he must stay at the edge of the room. When she hears him at the foot of the stairs, when she hears the front door close, she slips his money into her satin purse.

Alice waited. She blew on her fingers, her skirts were drenched; she had to dodge the drips running off the doorframe. But she waited until she saw John Motton's shape reappear behind the patterned glass, waited until she saw him quietly close the door, and turn back towards Kensington. She noticed a slight difference in his gait on his return journey.

And now she would do penance for her obsession. In exile from the Motton household she would design a series of hats for nurses and nuns, in the style of the French bonnets but less starched perhaps, more sympathetic. There would be bonnets and veils for different aspects of their work. Tomorrow she would visit the Sisters of Mercy at Marylebone; the day after, offer her services at St. Thomas's and St. John's.

Walking back to Kensington John Motton is warm, despite the cold rain. He is thinking about his paper for the *Review*, in which he planned to criticize Alexander Bain's declarations on what he called 'the unity of volition'; that is to say, 'will'. Bain's proposal, that the will's collective, muscular machinery was controlled by a distinct portion of the cerebrum, disposed to operate of its own accord, was in distinct contrast to the understanding of Combe, for whom, in practical terms, the will remained in the service of whatever feelings were uppermost in the mind. This is what John Motton knew, and in his new paper, he would point out at the start that Bain had made not a single anatomical study, not a single observation of individual behaviour—

No, Alexander Bain, you know nothing of Will, thought John Motton; whether or not there is a region in the cerebrum that contains Will, here was its manifestation: in not touching, never ever touching, the fragrant skin of one's mistress. In paying five guineas just to gaze at her, aroused almost beyond endurance. In paying one's mistress *eight* guineas to have her bind him up with a rope that cut his wrists; bind him to the iron bed and, with his eyes tightly covered, listen to her relieve herself into a pretty chamber pot. He likes this best. His hand moves towards his groin as he reaches the corner of his street.

As he unlocks the front door, he thinks he sees the back of Alice Heapy making her away along Silver Street. He darts inside and leans with his back against the door, listening for Mother, who lays in bed day after day, her face narrow, her eyes closed. And he allows his fingers to roam, thinking of Isabella, and Miss Alice Heapy with her irritating Puritanism, her endless questions, and his fingers press on the hard shape beneath the coarse wool.

Afterwards he goes upstairs to his father's room, takes one of his father's handkerchiefs from the old Draper's chest, unbuttons his trousers and wipes himself. He kneels down by the bed. He is crying, heaving, without making a sound. He gets up, opens the wardrobes, pulls out suit after suit, throws them on to the bed, the handkerchief still sticky and wet in his hand. He lies down over the garments, the worsted, the tweed, they scratch his face, and he begins to tear them, tear the arms from the sockets, to tear at the lapels and the buttons.

At dawn Mary, his servant, lets herself in downstairs. John Motton hears her, moves quickly into his own room and washes his face.

'Mary,' he walks calmly down the stairs. 'Mary, there's been a disturbance, an intruder—in Father's room. Please—yes, this way—dreadful business—kindly do not mention it to Mother, say nothing of it to Madam, it will only upset her.'

Mary begins to gather up the suits, the bow ties. Motton sees her blush as she finds the damp handkerchief: he knows she recognises that yeasty smell. He takes refuge in his Consulting Room. He gathers into his arms the papers from one side of the desk, almost cradling them: the notes for his paper on Alexander Bain and the proposed phrenological region of the Will. He draws them up to his face, and bangs them down on to the desk. He scatters the papers, lets them fall, and forces half of them into the wastepaper basket. He groans. Mary knocks at the door— all the time, Mary following him with her eye, listening as acutely as an animal. He flings open the door: 'Leave me alone.'

Mary has already vanished. He knows how often she has seen him like this; it has become more frequent in recent years.

At dawn that same morning, round the corner behind Kensington High Street, in her room overlooking the Laundry, Alice was lining up five blocks on the table under the window. She began to sketch the first headdress, for the nuns at prayer. Nuns must, she considered, have *Veneration* in the extreme, in the seventh degree, so that the organ that is situated in the middle of the sincipital region (the place that corresponds with the fontanel in children) would be prominent. Their current style, she had observed, was to have it discreetly covered with a soft muslin cap, pleated with a little crimping iron, and gathered close round their faces, underneath the starchy veil that pulled away from their faces. But the region should be exaggerated, she thought, and partially revealed. Her new design would bring the eye upwards to an open peak corresponding to the symbolic grandeur of the fontanel, and then flowing long but sharply away: rising and falling and rising, like Christ Himself.

The second bonnet would be for a nurse—a bonnet for the hope of recovery. This would be a fluted bonnet that would tend outwards away from the face and yet surround the face with light. Her natural countenance would be lifted, and the nurse would approach her patient with a gentle fluttering at her face and neck.

The third bonnet would be for the nuns to wear during the execution of their charitable works: looking after the orphans, training the older girls in needlework and laundry, visiting the sick. This bonnet would be lined in a special satin to give grace to the nuns' hard and exacting tasks, and the satin would be lined with goose down, a very fine layer, soft against each nun's closely cropped head.

The fourth, another nurse's headdress, would be a circle of silk for medical knowledge, fitted close on the scalp and from which muslin would fall in a medieval half-circle from behind the ears; muslin—to let the knowledge in and out.

The fifth hat would be a hat of darkness, the Hat of Black Grace, containing in embryo all the features of the other four hats: the one for prayer, with its peak; the one for hope, with its movement; the one for service with its satin and goose down; the one for knowledge with its circle of silk. But this one would be black and it would not be worn.

XI

Belinda Motton was sitting up in her bed. 'What is the matter with my son, Mary? He has been so disagreeable this week. I ask him to fetch one little thing for me and it is as if I have demanded he give up his profession to become my valet.'

'I suspect, Madam, that he is merely a little anxious about your health.'

'Ah, Mary—you are polite, but you surely know my son better than that? He is agitated, he is fretting—I have heard banging noises in the night, and that was after I had heard raised voices, when was it, the day before yesterday? He said it was Miss Alice Heapy, my milliner, and her brother, visiting. I said if Alice Heapy is here in our very house, then she should be up here discussing a new hat for me—why was he keeping her from me? Her hats are little miracles. My hat with the gauze ruffles—do you remember the day Alice brought it? How she pinned it on my head with her dexterous little hands, and when I saw my reflection in the mirror! I called Johnny straight away, of course—and he said, he said that I had been made angelic by the hat's fine gauze ruffles; made *radiant, no less,* by its layers of pale gold and lilac. "Mother," he'd cried out. "Look at you." And—don't you remember, Mary, he pulled me into his arms and danced me around the room. And then he upset poor Alice by shouting "Miss Heapy, you should make a transforming hat for yourself. You should give up that plain drab."

'But, you know, she is a funny little creature, Mary—so very *furtive.* If only she would allow Johnny to analyse her—like he did you, Mary. It helped you, didn't it? It helped you to understand… But Mary, listen: I say there is something the matter with my son. I know he is writing a paper, it's that Mister Bain—the *bane* of Johnny's life.' Belinda tittered into her hands.

'Perhaps he—' Mary hesitated. 'Perhaps he needs a wife, Mrs. Motton.'

'Good heavens, no. Mary, surely you understand that he is a *bachelor*? His father long ago discovered how very undeveloped was his son's *Conjugality.* My husband understood at once, that our son would never marry. He will never have a wife, Mary. Never. Now then, Mary, please, I need to rest.'

Mary was half way through the door when Belinda Motton called her back.

'Mary—ask Johnny to sit with me at lunch—I shall persuade him that my health would be singularly improved by having another splendid, sparkling new hat.'

XII

Alice was to make a hat for Mrs. Zaphinov's sister. Alice had never seen the woman before, but she understood she was a woman to be handled carefully.

The maidservant winked at Alice as she showed her into the drawing room—and there she was, Miss Linden of Bedford Gardens. Austere, the apartment rooms—no ornament, no relief from dark brown panels—and the woman, who sat in the room's shadows, the antithesis of her fountainous sister, wearing a table-brown jacket and skirt, almost invisible in her camouflage. She looked at Alice in silence for several minutes, during which time Alice became aware only of her own slovenliness, her broken fingernails, the glue on her sleeve. Miss Linden's dark brown eyes allowed no admittance; her thin lips formed a sneer in her long pale face. She did not ask Alice to sit down, nor make any gesture. Alice tried to remain steady under that ungracious gaze, thinking how she did not want to touch the oiled hair or the dreary neck as she should have to when she measured the woman: perhaps on this occasion she could simply estimate. Ah, she would willingly entertain four Mrs. Zaphinovs instead of this bitter oblong. As the image of four Mrs. Zaphinovs passed in front of Alice's eyes, Miss Linden spoke; a surprisingly high, thin voice, exhaling with each phrase. Alice noticed now that she had the deepest bosom she had ever encountered in her ladies, and as she spoke it was as if the breath was literally scaling its way up.

'Miss Heapy, I keep two bonnets, one for summer, one for winter. This year I require a new winter bonnet. It should be leghorn straw with a plain brown *bavolet*, exactly like that one on the table over there. Take it with you. Thank you, Miss Heapy, my maid will show you out.'

Alice stared at the bonnet. It was more than twenty years old. She picked it up and turned it over. Its light green lining was stained. She held it out against the shape of Miss Linden, realizing at once that its brim was too narrow for her great long face and that the green inside would lend a pallor over her skin. Without looking up, Alice told Miss Linden that it had been impossible to get leghorn straw since the 1848 trade wars in Europe.

'And anyway, I never work with straw.'

Miss Linden started up in her chair.

'*Madam*,' Alice added.

Her heart began to beat in her neck and hands. What was contained beneath the great bosom, what fury laid coiled there? Before Alice had time to find out, the maid came into the room, took the bonnet out of Alice's hands and ushered her out towards the front door, where she stopped, pressed the hat back into Alice's hands and winked at her once more.

'It's being spurned what does it,' she whispered. '*Spurned*, about fifteen years ago now. Her fiancé jilted her days before the wedding. Thought he'd be crushed to death by those great big—' She gesticulated over her own chest. Alice laughed, and put her hand over her mouth. 'She sees things now—she says to me that she *hall-u-cinates*, she says she sees the heads of flies and bits of their wings in front of her eyes, all that sort of thing. I've been here five years and all she's done is sit in that room like a mushroom. Suppose you thought you were going to make her a pretty little bonnet with all flowers and that, did you? Just give her what she wants, darlin', *or you'll regret it.*'

'Who was he?' asked Alice. 'Who was he, the fiancé?'

'I don't know. I don't even think he was a real one, you know, I think she *thinks* she was spurned.' The maid giggled. 'Come on, out you go, she'll be on at me otherwise. Bye-bye darlin'!'

Suppose, thought Alice, that John Motton was Miss Linden's jilting fiancé—the dates would fit, it would be shortly after his father died. He would have been distraught, he would want to punish himself, he would have sought a plain, solid woman who would allow him no movement, no grace. He would have wanted to suffer, to writhe in self-pity, and she would have been stern and punishing. Yet he would soon have been punished enough, he would grow to detest the way her lips made that incline away from him, and he would have made hurtful remarks to her, very quietly, so quietly that she would be uncertain as to whether she heard him correctly. And he would look away from her, in apparent contemplation but actually in contempt, plotting his escape. Of course she would have been slender then, she may even have had a pretty laugh, and her dark hair would still have had sunlight in it and her cheekbones would petticoat her eyes. She wouldn't have known a thing in those days: she would have worn her armour like a crocodile skin, scaly but magnificent. And he, John Motton—he would have been pleased by the slightly oily, fishy-oily texture of her, and by the silence between her few words. He would have liked the paternal aspect of the woman. John Motton, with his little bird mother, going towards this great father-rhinoceros of a woman. Or, maybe they were never betrothed but Miss Linden had some claim on the man, the result of some slight, a family feud, perhaps, whereby the Mottons owed something to the Lindens and the reparation was John Motton having to pay his respects repeatedly to the amphibian Miss Linden, and even occasionally to kiss the peach-skinned hand of Mrs. Zaphinov. And now he had replaced his desire with contempt, which was easier to bear, and he had bitterness: Alice knew him now. She knew, for example, that his contempt had forced his front teeth slightly apart, that it was his contempt that she could hear aspirating between those teeth. Yes, they all knew him now: Miss Linden, Alice's ally. And Mrs. Zaphinov, John Motton's sister-in-law? However would he sweep *her* up into a little chart, or indeed Miss Linden, the opposite of her sister: imposing but never incontinent, large but never extravagant; huge and oily and never to be seen in daylight?

'What do you mean, '*I'll regret it*'?' Alice shouted up from the bottom of the stone steps, but the maid simply touched her nose and closed the door and anyway, Alice knew exactly what she meant.

At home, Alice put Miss Linden's straw hat inside a hatbox and draped it over with remnants of black crêpe and parramatta. Then in an attempt to subdue these unwelcome and unwholesome speculations about the romantic life of Mr. John Motton, Alice worked with increased vigour on her series of hats for nuns and nurses. She took her little crimping iron and began to pleat her assembled pieces of white muslin. But soon she was full with questions once more, questions about how Motton perceived not the material world but an ideal world, where each person must be arranged and altered—and yet, what was wrong with self-improvement? What was wrong with Fowler's popular lectures at the Ludgate Institute?

There was a knock at Alice's door. It was Edward. He was wet. His beard was wet. She hugged him to her. He was clutching something—he had been to the Library, where he had copied out a page from *The Journal of the Phrenological Society* dated Autumn 1851, and he was thrusting the pages towards Alice. She could, he said, amuse herself during her exile from the Motton house by reading an article, an *obituary*, by her own Mr. John Motton, in which he described his late father, *Doctor* John Motton.

'Listen Alice, this is how the son describes the father: *His leading powers were Language, Individuality, Wit, Imitation,*

Marvellousness, Firmness, Self-Esteem, Love of Approbation, Secretiveness, Combativeness and Destructiveness. And what do we now know about the father, Alice? What do we now know?'

'That his head bulged here and was smooth there?'

'You see. Give me the Utopians! They will sooner tell us about Man,' cried Edward.

'But Edward, surely we know much about him from this description —Combative, Destructive, *Secretive*. Let us imagine the father, Edward, in order to understand the son. I have seen the wardrobes, I have seen the collection of yellow cravats—Mrs. Motton showed me, the collection of yellow cravats in a proper Draper's chest—fifty, a hundred yellow cravats! All of the best quality. All with little tags giving the name of the manufacturer, the price, the fabric.'

'But why must we bother ourselves imagining the lives of either John Motton or his father? And Alice,' Edward sat down on Alice's bed, 'you are much changed.' Edward looked at Alice's work table, at the white muslin in its tiny pleats.

'What is all this, Alice? Are these bridal headdresses? All this white?'

Alice stared at her brother. He clasped her hands. His hands were warm.

'And you are so thin, my dear sister. Perhaps you should come to stay with me and Cassandra—?'

'No, Edward. I am happy here. Look—this is where I am—Alice Heapy, Milliner—surrounded by all my drawings and tools and fabrics and—ideas.'

'Yes, Alice, so concentrate on your work. Let me and Cassandra deal with the Phrenologists.' Edward was smiling his sheep smile.

'Yes, Sir!' Alice saluted him.

He continued, 'And there are only two things I would say in favour of Phrenology: that in its early days, as Father explained to me once, it genuinely helped improve conditions for the criminal and the insane. And secondly, it allows us to rest in our beds knowing that our propensities are *not the result of our sin*, as the Christians would have it, but merely the result of an arbitrary placing in the structure of our skulls. What could be more reassuring?'

'And *less* reassuring, Edward. For it means that we need not take responsibility for our proclivities,' cried Alice.

'How does that follow? Phrenology surely says precisely the opposite. It says, rather, that we should take responsibility: first know your proclivities and then try to counter any imbalance, to work towards a state of equilibrium.'

Equilibrium. Alice thought of the hat that would bring her a state of equilibrium: a hat with puppet strings above and below.

'Go now, Edward. I must work.'

Edward kissed his sister's cheek. 'How cold you are, Alice.' He rubbed her arms.

'Go, dear brother. Or Cassandra will beat you with her parasol.'

Immediately Edward had left, Alice picked up the article from the *Journal*, written by John Motton, and imagined the terrible accident; the two men, the son and the father, arguing. The noise, the shouting, the horses' hooves, the screaming in the wet road.

Alice held in her hands a letter from Miss Linden. She studied the small masculine characters written in black ink. Would Alice please visit so that Miss Linden could order a platter hat for the spring? Alice had returned the old straw bonnet several days ago, handing it over to Miss Linden's maidservant with a note repeating what she had said originally—simply that she was unable to make Miss

Linden a straw bonnet. Alice fully expected retaliation, not capitulation. How was it that the scales had been lifted from the woman's amphibious eyes? Perhaps she too had found a beau, a military fellow, or a widower, a stocky clergyman from Manchester?

Alice would deliver her reply on the way to the Mottons': it would be her first visit since before Christmas. It was now February, and she could measure the weeks by the hats she had made: Miss Thirsk's wedding hat, Mrs. Zaphinov's lacy choux, the second hat in the Nuns and Nurses series.

'Come on in, Alice dear,' whispered Mrs. Motton, beckoning from the end of the hallway. Alice could hear John Motton's voice in the Consulting Room. 'Come on in,' repeated Mrs. Motton, clasping Alice's hands.

'You know, my dear, at the worst moments of my illness, I tried to imagine a row of new spring hats, to look ahead to a time when I could have you make me another new hat.' Alice was pleased. 'Now then, Miss Heapy, I suppose you have heard about Jemima Zaphinov's sister. It is less than a week since she was here in Johnny's Consulting Room, and can you believe it—previously a most unattractive woman, quite in the shadow of her marvellous sister—now the talk of the town: radiant, veritably *transformed.*'

Mrs. Motton exaggeratedly fanned herself with some gloves that she had plucked up from the table. They were silk, the colour of sloe berries. 'Dear Jemima is quite beside herself with her sister's ecstasy. Transformed—as I was for a little while when you made my cranberry and silk, when you, my dear, gave me gauze ruffles on lilac and gold. But, alas, I shall never, never get over the death of my dear husband, Alice dear—such a fine, respectable man he was. I have shown you his collection of silk scarves, cravats, haven't I? Imagine how fine they would have looked within dark lapels. Shall I show you his collection once more, my dear? Come upstairs, come this way.'

The last time Mrs. Motton talked of her husband precipitated Alice's exile from the Motton house. 'We have work to do, Mrs. Motton. I have another appointment this morning. Indeed, at Miss Linden's.'

'Good Heavens, my dear, what a coincidence. Well, let me show you quickly.'

Alice followed Belinda Motton up the stairs. They stood once more in front of the Drapers' chest.

'He loved to feel the silk on his fingertips, he was a—' she paused, 'he was a sensitive man, Miss Heapy.' A look of mock-coyness covered her face.

The cravats laid sultry with their fine tassels to the fore of the glass, each slightly overlapping the next, in an arrangement, Alice observed, that was slightly different to the one she had seen before. Alice imagined the man with a young, straight-backed Belinda Motton, the two of them passing the silks to each other, arguing lightly over which one her husband should wear.

'People are generally uninterested in widows, Miss Heapy, but you have taken an interest in me. And I want to tell you, to tell you that not a day goes by that I do not think of my husband. That I think of the love we had, of our life together. If it wasn't for my dear son I would have lost my mind long ago. You see, my husband and I, we were so perfectly matched. He kept me from—' She raised her eyes to the high ceiling. *From sailing up to the eaves,* thought Alice—'you know, Miss Heapy. But of course, I have my dear son, so clever, so highly respected. He has examined all my dear friends over the years: are *you,* Alice, are you not curious to know your special disposition, your mental proclivities?'

'I don't believe I have any special disposition or proclivities, Mrs. Motton.' Alice felt her cheeks redden.

'Nonsense, my dear. You have a very special talent: my son says that you are most unusual. It would be intriguing to know how, according to the special insights that only a Phrenologist may have, in what precise arrangement your faculties are combined. Mine for example: I have, as you would expect, very large *Philo*—can I even pronounce it—*Philo-progenitiveness,* 'love of one's offspring'—Johnny, my darling offspring. Here it is, at the back of my head—you will have felt it many times when you measured me, you have been covering it up with brims and flounces. Feel it now, dear.' Alice hesitated. Belinda Motton grasped her hand. 'See—it is combined with strong *Adhesiveness,* the love of home, and good *Self-Esteem* and *Firmness.* You know, it is this combination that makes me an excellent mother.

'Now dear, why don't you let him examine you? You should see how he has transformed Miss Linden—and he has often spoken of his admiration for your delightful millinery—and Miss Heapy, I suspect you are not always at ease? Mmm? Perhaps my son can bring you a little happiness by his expertise? As he has done for Mrs. Zaphinov's sister. Ah, I hear him now. Let us go downstairs at once and tell him you will be available for delineation, let us say, next Tuesday afternoon?'

'No, thank you, ma'am—I… There is nothing particular about me. I only know what my hands can do, how my eye informs my hands.'

'How very disingenuous of you, my dear,' replied Mrs. Motton, in a different tone, in a tone that Alice recognised from that early encounter when they had talked about Alice refusing to use straw. 'Come on, come with me.' And she led Alice firmly by the arm out of the bedroom and down the stairs, one definite, bony hand placed lightly between Alice's shoulder blades. John Motton was standing in the hallway, as if he was expecting them.

'Here she is,' cried Mrs. Motton.

Alice's instinct was to dart along the hallway and out of the front door, but John Motton's body was blocking her path; his co-conspirator urging her forward.

'Ah, Alice, come this way,' said John Motton. 'I have something I think you would be interested to see.'

Belinda Motton continued to ease Alice forward from behind and John Motton put his hand under her elbow. Together they steered her into the Consulting Room.

How long was it since Alice had been in the presence of John Motton? How long since she had followed him in the rain all the way to Holland Park and watched him slip in at a side door—? How long since she sat with Edward on the hard settee and endured humiliation?

'I thought Miss Alice Heapy, Milliner, should see one of Father's little eccentricities. Mother, you will remember this.'

On a low table sat a man's tall black dress hat, with a velvet nap. Motton scooped it up and turned it upside down. 'Look inside,' he commanded. Inside Alice could see what appeared to be ridges or slits, and a valve at the top of the crown. 'A ventilating hat,' said Motton, satisfied. 'See these cork channels? Look, the valve can be opened—to allow the wearer's perspiration to escape. It was Father's belief that insufficient ventilation was the cause of premature baldness. You see, Father was always most concerned that we should live strictly by the 'health-laws', that we should endeavour to take the right amount of fresh air, that we should avoid too much bitter and too much salt, that we should avoid spice, and too much heat. In all these small ways we may edge ourselves towards Perfection, to leading a Perfect life, Miss Heapy.' He put the hat back on the table and took Alice's hand. 'Now let's look at her, Mother. Don't you agree that she is rather pale, rather undernourished? Do you eat at *all*, Miss Heapy? Tell us, what are your favourite foods? Tell us, Miss Heapy, do you slavver over a juicy mutton-chop or a succulent steak pie, perhaps?'

'I wager she's a *Vegetarian*. Look, her skin is *powdery*.' Belinda cut in. 'Do you remember, Johnny, when Father insisted we all became Vegetarians. I had that little arrangement with Mary and the butcher—Father never knew a thing about it,' she tittered.

'Come Alice, come under the window.' He led Alice by the forearm. 'Mother—do you see a little yellowness in hue? Perhaps Miss Heapy has a slight liverishness?' He turned her shoulders this way and that for the light. She had become strangely powerless in their double presence; she had become their specimen.

'Yes, Johnny, I think I do. You had better sit down, Alice dear.'

Alice looked down. Beside her on the low table, next to the Ventilating Hat, was a pocket watch in a turquoise and gold embroidered case; there was a pack of playing cards in a maroon velvet sleeve; there were two large thermometers in orange silk cocoons. Alice sat down. 'Johnny' stood above her, behind her chair.

'Now, I believe I would locate not only powerful *Ideality* in this young woman,' said Motton to his mother, 'but also large *Individuality*—between your eyebrows, my dear—I refer to your powers of observation, your desire to see and examine. Such persons as possess this faculty in such a quantity are generally, if the right combinations allow—say, with large *Approbativeness* and *Self-esteem*—rather good judges of Character.' His lips thinned. 'Wouldn't you agree, Mother?'

'Certainly, Johnny,' cried Mrs. Motton. 'I am sure it is true, with Miss Heapy's gift for making hats that become us so.'

It was as if they could read her mind: her identified weakness, her inability to see Human Nature, or Character,

112

as a whole; her interest in the properties of only one element at a time; her obsession, for example, with the way a man could chew on a bit of gristle, without any thought as to what that might represent.

'She seems to have lost her tongue, Johnny. Perhaps you are thirsty, my dear? I shall call Mary to get some tea, dear. Mary! Mary! Oh, where is the blessèd girl? I shall have to go to the kitchen myself.'

'Remember, too, Alice, that some of your great strengths may not yet be apparent to you, not to the naked eye, of course. For example, I would imagine that under that very pretty hair you have large *Conscientiousness*, in other words, a strong desire to discover the truth: strong Integrity.'

'Sir,' Alice replied at last, picking up the playing cards. 'That may well be true, and all of these things about myself I have observed already. Surely I do not need—'

'You may be aware of your strengths, Alice, but many of us are much less cognizant of our weaknesses.' He knelt on one knee in front of her. 'You may or may not have insight into their exact configuration in your brain. And Madam, you need to understand the nature of your *weaknesses* even more than your strengths. Remember, Phrenology promises us control over our lives, by understanding our weaknesses. I suggest you would indeed benefit from a little more control over your life?'

Control over you, Sir. 'But, Sir—' Alice could not in fact disagree with the man.

'Now, I propose that some of those weaknesses are making you unhappy, my dear.' He took Alice's hands in his. 'And that you, like all of us, desire moral perfection—it is what we all wish for. It is what we all aspire to, however *secretly.*'

A tear slipped out of Alice's eye. She wrest her hands from his and turned her face away. Still he went on.

'You see, Alice, Phrenology teaches us what we are and what we are capable of becoming—but to be exact I would need to make close and repeated examinations, followed by rigorous interpretation.'

Please do not do this, Mr. Motton. I shall not surrender.

'I am your mother's milliner, Sir, it is best that—'

The door was opening and a tea tray emerging. Motton stood up. 'And how is that young brother of yours, Miss Heapy?' He patted the top of his head. 'Still up here with the Utopians?' But Alice was dashing out of the room, out into the street, along Church Street and Bird Walk and away amongst the stalls and dark cloth and awnings and papers and wet dirt. Away.

Miss Linden's maid greeted Alice on the top step. She looked at Alice with wide eyes and tapped the side of her head. Then she flung open the drawing-room door, to reveal Miss Linden standing at the French windows. *And her face did shine as the sun; and her raiment was white as the light.* She was wearing pearl-pink, probably an outfit belonging to her sister—indeed for a moment Alice believed it was Mrs. Zaphinov herself. The pink dress had folds and tucks at the front, the deep white bosom revealed its cleavage, and the skin above was decorated with an elaborate coral necklace. She was framed by new blue-gold harlequin curtains, and there was an expression on her face that surely represented a smile.

'Mr. Motton has examined me,' Miss Linden said, 'and do you know what he has found?' Miss Linden began, without the usual formalities.

Alice looked down at her hands.

'Mrs. Belinda Motton's son, Mr. John Motton: I believe you and he are acquainted?' *Acquainted, yes.* 'Well, Miss Heapy, John Motton has found that I have *Wonder* in the greatest degree. He deduced from this fact that I should no

114

longer hide myself away. Thus I am renewed, re-valued, like a jewel found on the riverbed and kept in a drawer with no-one previously knowing its true worth. Wonder, my dear, *Wonder*! It means, as the excellent Mr. Motton explained, that my deepest desires are for that which is marvellous— the miraculous, the unexpected, the grand, the extraordinary and of course, at this level, the *Sublime*.'

Alice continued to look at her hands.

'Do you hear me, Miss Heapy? I am in the company, in this aspect, Mr. Motton says, of none other than Socrates, Joan of Arc, and Mister Oliver Cromwell.'

She stepped out from the window frame and bent towards Alice, her long face looming. Alice stepped back.

'*Wonder*, my dear; and so I issue you with a challenge, Miss Heapy, to create a hat that will both suit, and moreover, *embody*, my dear Miss Heapy, *embody* this: my *transformation*.'

Miss Linden had not invited her to sit down, and Alice found herself leaning against the piano, sitting on its stool, her hat and gloves still on, her face burning. 'Tell me more, Miss Linden, tell me more about your *transformation*.'

The word in Alice's own head was the more religious one, trans*figuration*, and yet she couldn't help but feel irritated by the pride Miss Linden now exhibited. She seemed to have absorbed a bit of that same pride that filled the shoulders and pulsating neck of John Motton. Miss Linden had been transformed, even transfigured, by John Motton, but Alice thought she preferred the woman in her misery cloak, surrounded by her oak panels. The light on Miss Linden came from the outside, and it was dazzling.

'What is the matter, Miss Heapy, are you not pleased for me?'

Alice did not answer but rose up now and moved swiftly towards Miss Linden, snatching her measure out of her pocket and whipping it round Miss Linden's head. She whispered in Miss Linden's ear, 'What is your Christian name, Madam? It would help me to know.'

'Ah, it is Alicia—a pretty name, don't you think? Alicia Linden.'

Alice drew back. 'Stand absolutely still for one moment, would you mind, Ma'am?'

She measured the distance between the woman's crown and the nape of her neck, recoiling at the musty smell of her, which hadn't been transformed. She looked at Miss Linden's ears from behind, and laid her hands on the woman's hair. *I touch the place where Wonder lies, directly above Amativeness, and with each of my hands I cover the sections that pulsate, just above Miss Alicia's ears. Secretiveness; surely there is Secretiveness here.* The woman was a little uneasy: Alice's movements were too sudden, too near.

And then, a tap at the door, and in swept Mrs. Zaphinov, wearing her lacy choux.

'Ah, Alicia—good heavens above, look at you. The butterfly out of her dark chrysalis. And all the work of Belinda's boy, I gather. Miss Heapy, *you* know the fellow.'

Mrs. Zaphinov swirled about the room, looking at her sister from every angle. Miss Alicia Linden twirled to give her sister the better view. Alice was caught in between the swirling and twirling of the huge-bosomed sisters: she became the slender body of a pink and peach butterfly with outsize wings.

'Let me make my appointment,' cried Mrs. Zaphinov. 'I must be examined at once by the gentleman who can bring radiant happiness to the most miserable of women. And why not have him examine you, Miss Heapy? Let him examine all the women in London!'

When Miss Linden had arrived in the Consulting Room, after Mrs. Motton had clapped her hands and congratulated Alicia Linden on the wisdom of her decision to be examined, John Motton had remained behind his desk for as long as possible, gathering up all his masculine strength to meet the force of the woman. His heart sank as he first approached Miss Linden, for he knew that neither this woman nor his mother would want a set of results that genuinely and accurately described Miss Linden's proclivities. But, as he made his way towards Miss Linden's great bosom, his eye had caught the word 'Wonder' on the porcelain head, and at once he began to enthuse, to move round Miss Linden with a semblance of awe, and on putting down his callipers, took a red handkerchief from his pocket and wiped his brow.

'It is remarkable, Madam, truly remarkable,' he had begun, and pausing in his remarks whilst he measured and calculated some more, stood back a little—thought what a clever actor he was—and finally whispered the word 'Wonder' so quietly that Miss Alicia Linden had to lean towards him, anxious, but reading on his face that he had discovered something special, possibly unique, in her configuration.

And afterwards, to his horror, she had become the talk of the town, telling all who would listen how he had transformed her with his skill and brilliance; and he thought how his father would condemn those Phrenologists who surrendered their professional integrity to clients they feared.

So when Miss Linden's sister, Mrs. Zaphinov, demanded he examine her as well, he instructed his mother and Mary to delay her. 'For I really must complete the final revisions to my paper on Alexander Bain,' he told them, and began to think once again about the nature of the human will, about volition and control, and wondered if he might yet be able to retrieve a few ideas from an old notebook. Then he thought of the white skin and the dark nipples of his mistress, which he had not once allowed himself to touch. He began to think also of Alice Heapy; that if only she would allow him to examine her, he would be able to trace, to decipher every con tour of her sensuality; that he would discover in her a fresh young libertine.

Alice decided to work through the night on Miss Linden's designs. Her fingers were numb inside her fingerless work-gloves; the glass in the window was cracked and a tiny hole let in a Siberian wind. In an attempt to keep her head warm she wore a turban, a rolled, coiled dough-hat made from felt, like the Bedhouin hats from the last century. She had seen books, books her mother had shown her, techniques of millinery, drawings of hats from the world over. There was no shape, no fabric, with which she was not familiar.

She brought out her brown paper and tracing papers from under the bed; she sharpened her black pencils. There would be three hats to choose from, and they would each contain a secret: each would have pockets inside, pockets that had cavities but no openings. Each would have a pocket that would sit over Miss Linden's two special Phrenological sites, *Wonder*, given by Mr. John Motton, and *Secretiveness*, given by Miss Alice Heapy. Not only would there be pockets in Miss Linden's hats, but words, which Alice would write on tiny rectangles of white silk, using pins dipped in dye to scratch the surface. The words would be, simply, the Phrenological terms, *Amativeness*, for example. Alice conjugated it: *Amativeness, Amativo, Amativa, Amatitarti, Amatarten, Amati-amen.* No definitions, simply the words, for they would look beautiful in pin-dye writing, scratched, as if breathed upon the silk. They would rest there inside the pockets, which would be made of thin velvet. Earlier that day Alice had gathered up all sorts of pieces at Nash's and slipped them up into her sleeves. She had studied her tongue in the shop mirrors: the velvet of the pockets was the colour of the tip of Alice's tongue.

The shape of the hats was significant, for concealment must have the right shape. It must be bowed, there must be an arc; concealment must have a bold shape, for wasn't it the case that concealment afforded power? Wasn't that something that Miss Alicia Linden had discovered? Wasn't that the reason why her bosom had become great, because she concealed her heart, more than any other organ? For the heart beat, it was visible, it appeared here in her wrist, in her throat; it made a sound, it *exposed* her; it was a manifestation, and it *must be concealed.*

The height of the hats, Alice decided, would be approximately eighteen inches up from the crown of the head, but she might revise the height after she had measured Miss Linden once more. She needed more exact measurement, she must not be wrong; she should make her own milliner's callipers, an adaptation, an invention to be patented, a dainty, polished wooden pair—walnut, perhaps—which she would keep with her scarlet pincushion in a purple leather box with a gold silk lining.

Now shape: what other shape would suit an oblong? Alice looked at the reflections in the black of her window: shapes to suit an oblong with *Wonder* and concealment in equal measures—and she thought of the Taj Mahal; and then a series of Bedouin tents; and two fish going separate ways, Parting Fish. Here then, *Wonder*, and concealment, which had made itself manifest, present in all the pockets.

In the past Alice's desire had been to bring balance, to bring harmony. But that was before John Motton had crouched down before her and promised to disclose her weaknesses. Now she only wished the human proclivities to be exaggerated, to be expanded and indulged; to be exaggerated even to the point of death. For all is better than exhortation, she said to herself; all is better than the attempt to alter that which Nature has made manifest.

So Miss Linden would have a Taj Mahal hat that would be delicately lifted by wire, a pirouette of pearls with white and pink sequins directing the eye to the pinnacles. The base would be two inches deep, made from a band of watermarked gold ribbon, and the band would be lined with the thin velvet. It should feel soft against Madam's brow—Alice wanted Miss Linden to know comfort. And she would place some of her pin-scratched silk pieces inside, between the band of gold ribbon and the tongue-pink velvet.

Or perhaps Miss Linden should have the Tent series, made from a type of desert canvas. This hat would be constructed once again by wire, it would be a geometry of three Bedouin tents the colour of sand; sand flies would be embroidered over the hat with iridescent thread. Alice would go to the Library and make drawings of sand flies from pictures in the books. They would be mating, laying eggs, they would glow and die, but the stitches would be so small that none of these things would be visible except under a magnifying glass, and Alice had never known anyone yet to take a magnifying glass to a hat.

Or perhaps it should be Parting Fish: two fat, silver, gold and turquoise fish, each taking a secret away in different directions? Alice was reminded of Mother and Edward: they were once again on the green satin sea, with fish going this way and that, fish like their hearts, Alice's and Edward's, going in different directions. They had to go separately, like Miss Linden's Parting Fish; they had to go away from the secret of their mother. Alice worked through the night, waiting for the sun to rise.

XIII

As the sun was rising, Edward came up to Alice's room, on the way to his work. Alice had not slept at all and now she was sitting on her bed curling feathers. Edward sat down next to her, his hands clutching his temples.

'She will not let it rest, Alice. She drives at me constantly. She comes into the workshop at lunchtime, bringing me a quite unnecessary sandwich and proceeds to harangue me for half an hour whilst I am endeavouring to plane or chisel or press. She is insufferable. And a terrible feeling wells up in me, in my throat, when she is at her antics. I cannot forgive her, for she cannot be satisfied by what I am.'

'It is cruel,' said Alice, picturing the quite unnecessary Cassandra.

'I thought I could put up with any insult, any defamation, for the sake of having the warm body of that woman next to mine at night. Well, and so did I until...' Edward stood up.

'Cassandra has a *friend*, Alice—a *man-friend*. He was a railway engineer until he signed up for the Ludgate course. Can you believe it, Alice, it really is called "Become a Phrenologist in Ten Days" and now he has clients queuing up outside his house, and the people coming out after their sessions are almost mobbed. I am certain she is in love with the man, for she says *Walter* this and *Walter* that until I could ram his callipers down his throat.' Edward thumped Alice's worktable. 'And Alice, you know, she has that— passionate body and she *keeps* it from me. I am insane with wanting her, yet I can hardly bear to speak to her—we are at war. Yes, we are at war!'

Alice put her hand on Edward's shoulder, and the two remained in silence. Finally, Edward looked at his sister.

'Alice, you are very pale.' Alice took his hand and laid it on her cheek.

'Poor Edward,' she said.

'Of course,' Edward continued, 'of course, as soon as I realised the *truth*, I resolved at once to remain a blocker after all, never again to be pulled off track by my faithless wife.'

'She will love you again soon, Edward,' said Alice, *when it is all over, when Phrenology has finally been forgotten.*

'So in the meantime I must carry on toiling by day so that Cassandra may purchase mass-produced parasols, and reading the socialist philosophers in the evenings whilst she cuckolds me with a Ten Day Phrenologist called Walter! Is that what you would advise, Alice? Is it?'

'I cannot help you, Edward. I am too tired,' she said. But through Edward's talking Alice had begun to make a plan, a plan that involved a different kind of 'cuckolding'— she would have her head analysed, but not by John Motton. She would go to the Phrenologist named on Miss Thirsk's card: Dr. Firbank.

The church clock was chiming. Edward kissed Alice's forehead and went out of the door, his shoulders more hunched than ever. A minute later he came back. He handed Alice a book. 'I forgot to give you this.' It was Darwin's *Origin of Species.* Alice stopped curling the feathers and began at once to read the book, thinking back to that occasion with John Motton when she had foolishly announced that Darwin represented the pinnacle of our understanding of human nature, or some such thing that she had heard from Edward's lips.

Later, Mary came to her door. She handed Alice a white card. Here it was then, confirmed in Motton's own hand, the date and time of her Appointment: a week Tuesday, at half-past five in the afternoon. She wrote a letter to Dr. Firbank.

*

Alice had no coal. She could not get warm. She was too cold to work. There were new shards of ice in her bowl. She thought of John Motton examining all the women in London, laying his manicured hands on their shoulders, turning them this way and that. She brought out all her fabrics and placed them on top of the bed: Irish flax, Duchesse satin, the plain white muslin for the nuns and nurses. She got into the bed, and laid a piece of fine Merino wool over her face. She tried to sleep. It was three o'clock in the afternoon. She didn't know whether she was awake or asleep. It was six o'clock. Alice was awake. She put on two dresses and her cloak. She would go to her beautiful Miss Thirsk. She did not need the knowledge a man could give, after all: she would be in thrall, instead, to a woman.

Miss Thirsk greeted Alice without surprise. It was warm. Miss Thirsk was warm; she had been sitting by the fire, by the reckless, wanton, blazing fire. She took her box of chess pieces on to her lap. 'Will you play, dear Alice?' She lifted the Chinese figures slowly out of the box and into position on the board. She spent a few moments making sure each piece sat exactly in the centre of its square.

She no longer mentioned the rotund gentleman who must reach tall to touch her swan-feather neck. Alice could not know the precise circumstance of his demise but she suspected that he had been quite unable to meet the necessary level of restraint. Perhaps Miss Thirsk had discovered his perspiring palm on her bare shoulder, in front of the peat fire (Alice could imagine Miss Thirsk's small smile as he left). Miss Thirsk knew he would eventually have to relinquish her, and that she would again smile her wistful smile, for the men who believed she had a sadness about her of which she never spoke. Open on the chair was the poem by Algernon Charles Swinburne, 'Chastelard'.

'Do you know it? It is a poem in which the hero is a slave to a passion for a woman he despises,' she said. 'I'd like to see if the Phrenologists could lash Swinburne down with their formulations.' She laughed darkly in her alto voice. Alice saw that she was using Dr. Firbank's card as a bookmark. 'Now,' said Miss Thirsk 'let us move a few of these pieces, then we shall have a little brandy.'

The two women faced each other over the green and turquoise marble figures. Then Alice saw it. Inside a glass cabinet sat Miss Thirsk's special hat for being carried to the county of Cork: Alice's little jay, its beak glistening in the light of the fire, its legs azure and gold. Ah, Miss Thirsk—she had *Wit*, she had *Mirthfulness*, in the largest degree! The women pushed the figures towards each other on the board. Alice was in thrall to a woman.

Miss Thirsk poured brandy into dusty glasses. She put the chess table aside, brought a long piece of printed silk and laid it over the rug by the fire. She knelt down, beckoning Alice to join her on the printed silk by the fire. 'Let *Amativeness* be our single propensity,' she whispered. They sipped their brandy, they slid down on to the silk, they stroked each other's arms. Miss Thirsk was so warm, the fire so reckless and wanton. Miss Thirsk pressed her fingers over Alice's lips.

Alice had an appointment. She walked all the way to Farringdon in another face-sucking wind, across Marble Arch, on to Clarendon, whipped by her plan for revenge. Revenge, when she had yet to be properly aggrieved. But *he* had been stealing her mind, a private part of her that did not even know itself. If she were to be in thrall to a Phrenologist, let it be not John Motton but the one recommended by Miss Thirsk and Miss Thirsk's aunt; let it be the one whose visiting card kept Miss Thirsk's place in the pages of Swinburne's 'Chastelard'.

The door was level with the street, black and splashed with mud. Its brass knocker was tarnished. Alice lifted the knocker and tapped twice. The door opened to reveal a voluminous, theatrical, purple coat. High up, from its ruff collar emerged a lined narrow face made wide by white whiskers. Alice whispered her name and Dr. Firbank nodded. He looked kind. His coat swished as he turned back down the hallway, leading Alice into a dusty panelled room and sitting her down in front of the fire. Alice watched the man as he fished in his voluminous coat like a magician, bringing forth the callipers, then the tape measure and the consulting chart, and the pen, and the ink. She watched him as if she were his apprentice. It seemed that he had pockets of different sizes and strengths sewn inside his coat to carry all the materials that a Phrenologist might need. Perhaps he would in a moment bring out from the satin lining a porcelain head. But there was no head, no head anywhere in the room.

All the instruments were in place and Dr. Firbank faced Alice. The whiskers met his eyebrows and in his tiny silver eyes was an image of the fire. Alice sat on a straight-backed chair with her knees slightly to one side. At last his liver-spot hands came trembling from his white frilled cuffs and Alice wondered how these hands could ever make an accurate reading. She thought how she used to entertain a desire to have Motton's smooth hands on her; instead this mottled and wobbling pair was approaching her, now level with her chest, now level with her shoulders. But he did not touch her head. First, he picked up one of her hands, tugged at the fingertips of her glove, eased the glove off and laid it down next to the array of instruments.

'You are cold, Madam.'

'Yes, Sir, I have walked from Kensington.'

He rubbed Alice's hand between his bony pair, blowing on her fingertips. It seemed to be the case, then, that all

Phrenologists felt entitled to touch, to stroke, to hold the hands of their female clients. And so Alice could begin to generalise about Phrenologists. She could begin to compare Dr. Firbank, with his enlarged Adam's apple rising and falling above the starched collar, with the herringbone pillar that was Mister John Motton. And yet this Dr. Firbank had tried to warm her hands; there was tenderness in the man.

But now he was approaching, tall and ungainly in his swishing velvet coat, with the callipers in one hand and his notebook in the other. He was coming as if he would brand her with gleaming callipers.

'Dr. Firbank!' She must interrupt his advance. 'Dr. Firbank, I wish to ask a question.' He was statuesque, his bony face with the hook nose was angled towards her. 'Doctor, don't you wish to know my name, my age, my personal details before you take the measurements?'

'My dear girl—there is nothing of significance except the measurements and their interpretation. Nothing of significance. Therefore I assess your physiology first, and last.' His tongue stuck on the s's, there was saliva around the hard c's in the middle of his words. His lips were as wet and soft as a baby's.

Alice thought of Miss Linden, who had been transformed by a Phrenologist. She thought of the dark, oily woman who had become light and dry. She thought of how Miss Linden had taken Wonder into herself and become radiant, apparently by this process, in the presence of a Phrenologist, like this one, who was arriving now, faster than before, his callipers were upon her head, he was placing the instruments over her skull, he was moving her hair with his shivering hands, stopping only to write down numbers in a notebook. It was a violation: she was but a set of numbers, written in tight forward-slanting script. *He is measuring me. He will cut my life short.* Alice stood up.

'Madam, we are not complete.'

'I am complete, Sir.'

His hand landed on Alice's shoulder as if from a great height. She sat. He measured, he wrote in his notebook. She wept. The fire formed images: Mrs. Zaphinov in the hallway; John Motton in his ginger wool; Mrs. Motton's feathers; the wings in front of Miss Linden's eyes; Miss Thirsk. Dr. Firbank was hissing, talking to her, he was saying, Miss Heapy, we are complete. He had laid down his callipers on the table. He had replaced the notebook with his payment book. Alice was handing him the four guineas and his Adam's apple was still. She gazed up at him, still seated on the hard chair around which he had moved noiselessly, standing back, getting close, and then moving away. She was the centre of his mind world; she was his object, his subject, his pretty prey. She was neither woman nor milliner: she was the calculations for the proof of a theory. She prayed now that her sincipital region had contracted at the sight of Firbank's predatory hands, and that other regions had expanded to become baggy and loose. She should have breathed space into her temples and forced her eyebrows apart. She would have laughed for its absurdity. But she had fulfilled her mission: she had been *unfaithful;* unmarried, she had committed adultery. Mr. John Motton could never claim her now for his virgin-bride.

The old man said he would post the results in the morning. Alice feared that in his frailty he would confuse his notes of her reading with that of another patient, and that her destiny would be permanently altered, just as she had imagined John Motton 'putting her back wrongly'. And as she edged down the hallway to the front door, she realised that could indeed be the answer: to spend the rest of her life correcting faults that she did not have.

XIV

Alice waited three days, six days for Dr. Firbank's results. They did not come. She decided to visit Mrs. Zaphinov, for ballast, and because she had been neglecting her. Surely Mrs. Zaphinov would like another meringue hat for visiting the wives of Members of Parliament. Or indeed, as the great woman's body seemed to be constantly evolving, migrating, even, then Alice would honour Mrs. Zaphinov with a series of Darwinian hats, with Hats for the miracle of Evolution. This was how they would be:

A series of five, a procession; they would be laid out on a track so that they were discreetly moveable. They would feature colours from the newest and most brilliant dyes available. They would have within them, inside the crowns, silken clouds and arcs of sunrays. They would be stitched with luminous thread, not in the shapes of animals or insects or birds or fish this time but with a representation of the sounds made by the different species. Thus Alice would prop open her father's book about Darwin's adventures on the HMS Beagle and embroider a call, a gurgle, a mating cry and the rattle of a cricket.

Or, if Mrs. Zaphinov said she didn't want the Darwinian hats, then Alice would make instead a Spectroscope Magnifying Hat, much superior even to Dr. John Motton's old Ventilating Hat. This one would be made from a matrix of prisms that enabled one to see a one millionth part of a grain of sodium. It would magnify by one million the beautiful curls on the head of Mrs. Zaphinov. It would be a hat for the magnification of the propensities, a hat for Exaggeration. A hat for Alice's surrender, for today was Thursday and Tuesday was the day that Alice would have her Reading with the great, the revered, the *wonder*ful John Motton.

But before Alice ran up Campden Street to Mrs. Zaphinov's house, she would dress in white muslin, place a band of white muslin over her eyes, keep it in place for half an hour; let whiteness enter her soul.

'What is the matter, Mrs. Zaphinov? Shall I draw the curtains?'

'The matter *is*, Miss Heapy, that I am in the presence of a madwoman. You frighten me, Miss Heapy, with your antics. I simply want another sumptuous meringue or a glamorous lacy choux for afternoon tea with the wives of Members of Parliament. But you, Miss Heapy, you come here dressed in white muslin in the middle of winter—for it is not Spring yet, and look at your skirts—*filthy!* Why do you come here to torment me with ideas for hats which can never be realised?'

But she seemed motherly in her reprimand: she gave Alice a mass, a wall, an opposite; she gave Alice a beginning and an end. Alice would continue to describe the Ark series of hats, for she liked this feeling of containment within the woman who spilled, who frothed, who roared.

'And,' Mrs. Zaphinov continued, swatting at Alice with her gloves, 'my sister twirls round London with a golden halo on her head, whilst I have been quite unable to make an appointment with the very important John Motton. Even though I said to Belinda, tell him I am Mrs. *Zaphinov*. Has the man never heard of my late husband? But no, far too occupied writing some paper or other. So all I have is *you*, Miss Alice Heapy, and my dogs. Where are my dogs? Pupps! Lapkins! Pupps!'

When Mrs. Zaphinov finally swept into John Motton's Consulting Room, filling it with perfumes and powders and rolling yards of peach-pink chiffon, Motton puffed himself up and decided at once that the woman urgently required constraint; of course he didn't need get his callipers out of their box to know that this was a case of huge and perverted *Alimentiveness,* a case of extreme gourmandizing and gluttony. Moreover, *Self-Esteem* was grotesquely distorted, causing degrees of pomposity and superciliousness that veered completely off the Phrenological scale. In response to his hostility, Mrs. Zaphinov swelled up even more, ballooned to the very edges of his Room.

And when she received the results—despite the protestations of both Belinda Motton and Mary, for he was on the very cusp of finishing his paper on Alexander Bain—she swept into his Room once more, a dog under each arm. Before he could speak, Mrs. Zaphinov had seated herself in front of John Motton's desk and begun her tirade:

'You bestow my sister Alicia with *Wonder* but *I* must suffer humiliation. Why, you wish to contain me, to restrict me,' she declared. 'Young man, *I* am Mrs. *Zaphinov,* yet you would strap my arms to my sides with your look. You seem quite unable to comprehend that it is a good thing, yes, a virtuous thing, for a woman to be voluptuous and sumptuous like me. Yes, I choose peach, I choose apricot, I want my scent to be most floral. I delight in chiffon and lace and little pet dogs. Yes, I shall tie the ribbon-bows for small dogs until Kingdom Come!'

Motton gazed at the scene in front of him: Mrs. Zaphinov had her two small dogs in her lap, stroking their silken ears with her silk glove, smoothing away at their bow-tied forelocks.

'I believe you do not like dogs, Mister Motton, not my dogs, nor any dogs. Ah, but no-one shall judge me except my dogs, and if I am lacking, only *they* will be correct in chastising me. Come on, Pupps. Ah, I will stroke your ears, ah, your silken ears, let me furnish your bow, ah, Mummy loves Pupps. C'mon, c'mon, here's my smooth lap for you, smooth lap.

'And of course you asked me about my hat, and when I told you that it was made by Miss Alice Heapy, you became tense and, I thought, a little spiteful in your movements, yet Miss Heapy is a milliner who can make a hat as luxurious and as delicate as meringue, she is the only woman in the trade who can do it, and I need her. Yes, I need that little purse-lipped, hiding-in-corridors girl with her tiny face and fancy ideas. Of course, she thinks she is above the rest of her class, with her prim little notions. She is an aesthete, she is a sorceress, and I would keep her sewing meringues and tiered wedding cakes until she has barely a breath left in her. And I gather now that you, Mr. John Motton, are familiar with Miss Heapy. Of course, she imagines she is invisible, when in fact we can all see her antics. Since my last visit to you, Mister Motton, she has come strangely to me wearing swathes of white muslin, talking of Evolution and mating calls and Flying Spectroscopes, for Heaven's Sake! She is a sorceress, I tell you, and we all need her, we need her mad little ways for she can make a meringue to lay flat on top of my curls, eh Pupps? She can do it, eh Pupps, yes, only she can do it.

'But *you*, Belinda Motton's son, have tricked me and done me a disservice, for I do not understand how *Alicia* has been transformed and not I.'

At last, Mrs. Zaphinov stopped talking. Now she simply breathed noisily and petted her two little dogs. John Motton walked over to the window and with his back to Mrs. Zaphinov, asked, 'Talking of Evolution and mating calls and Flying Spectroscopes?'

'You see how she agitates you, Mr. Motton, our milliner,' replied Mrs. Zaphinov. 'How she agitates us all!'

*

Mrs. Peake slipped an envelope under Alice's door. It did not contain the Firbank results. It was an Invitation. It was Belinda Motton's birthday—Alice must join a small party on Saturday afternoon. Alice had her two beautiful secrets now; and she would attend the small birthday party of Mrs. Belinda Motton.

It was half-past four. Alice was wearing cobalt blue. She had her hair a little loose. She didn't like stern best; today she liked loose.

Mary opened the door. She was holding a red balloon on a gold ribbon. 'Madam is in the dining room—and there's someone she wishes to introduce to you,' she said with a curious twist of her chin. Alice followed Mary and the red balloon towards the dining room. Mary took the unusual step of announcing her. And there she was: magnificently red and brocadely black, standing in the window with Belinda Motton.

'Ah, Alice Heapy!' cried Mrs. Motton, '*So* delighted you were able to come this afternoon. Isabella, this is my little Milliner, a most talented young woman. Now, Alice dear, Mrs. Raleigh has much admired the hats you have made for me. Mrs. Raleigh would also like to commission a hat.'

Mrs. Raleigh studied Alice. Alice curtseyed, moving backwards. Mrs. Raleigh's hair was shining black. Her lips were red. She was tall, and broad. She was regal. Belinda Motton was speaking again.

'Isabella is the daughter of one of my late husband's professional acquaintances and she truly *adores* my cranberry silk. She would like something similar—although not *too* similar, of course.' She emitted a squeak and patted Isabella's arm.

Alice's lips shrank. 'Ma'am,' she said, knowing the meaning of the word 'sullen.' Isabella wanted a cranberry bonnet: she would not have one; instead she could have sour sloe berries. Mrs. Raleigh was looking down at her gloved hands, the gloves reached high up her arms. She can smell me, thought Alice.

'Mrs. Raleigh is staying with her aunt who is an invalid. The poor woman cannot be disturbed by callers, so she asks that you measure her here, after tea, my dear.' *It appears that Mrs. Raleigh cannot speak for herself.* 'Now, Johnny has a measure you may borrow, or perhaps you carry one about your person at all times. Mary!'

Mary came into the room. She had tied the red balloon to her wrist with the golden ribbon.

'Bring in the birthday cake at once, and fetch Johnny— ask him to bring his measuring tape.'

John Motton arrived, wearing swallow-tails and a red and gold spotted bow-tie. He was handsome: tall, and broad. He was carrying the cake on one hand, level with his shoulder. It was a reckless pyramid of *choux*, piled high on a glassy plate, and he walked ceremoniously towards the dining table, which was laid over with a lacy cloth. Mrs. Motton clapped and cooed. Mrs. Raleigh bowed her head lightly. Mary stood at the edge of the room with an inexplicable fullness in her lips.

'Let us sit at the table,' John Motton shouted out. 'Mary, you must sit with us today! Mother! You are to sit at the head of the table. Isabella, you will sit next to me, here. Alice Heapy, you will sit opposite, here, next to Mary. Come on, ladies, come on now.'

The women assembled. They took up their napkins and laid them over their laps.

'I shall cut the cake,' he said. 'Pass me your plates.'

The plates were decorated with miniature blue pagodas and ornate bridges. Mary poured tea into the cups. The rim of Alice's cup was painted gold and fluted—she couldn't quite place her lip flush at its edge, so that her lips also became fluted and she feared the tea would roll away down the tiny funnels and on to the lacy cloth. At the bottom of her cup there would be a cluster of blue clouds edged with an arc of sunrays.

After the tea, after the spectacle of John Motton and Isabella Raleigh sitting close together, after the pattering and twittering of Belinda Motton throughout, after Alice's awkward measuring of the magnificent Isabella Raleigh with John Motton's measure, John Motton took Alice into the hall and said in his wisp-wasp voice, 'My dear Alice,' slightly lisping the soft 'c' in her name, 'you didn't answer my letter, inviting you for your reading. Allow me to suggest that I believe you have a most interesting cranial configuration and that it is far from usual to encounter a woman of such exceptional *Constructiveness*. On Tuesday, you will be having your head analysed for the sake of posterity, for the good of scientific development. It will be over within an hour, and then you will be free, free to go back to your hats. You also desire this knowledge, my dear.'

Alice blushed. Alice blushed not for John Motton's attentions, but for the memory of Dr. Firbank's reading. John Motton believed her head to be virgin, that his reading would chart new territory. She blushed a little more and smiled; he would think she was almost persuaded.

'Next Tuesday, then, Alice,' he said. 'As arranged, I shall see you at half past five.'

'I am a milliner, Sir; I have much to do.' It wasn't possible to get past him to the door, for he was blocking the hallway; she could neither see above him nor beyond him. He would not end this awkward proximity.

Isabella Raleigh had asked Alice to decide upon a style of hat that would suit her. The woman did not herself seem to have an opinion; and then Alice realised: she had asked

Alice to decide, to act on her instincts so that Alice would reveal *herself*, reveal *her* weaknesses.

Alice walked to Kensington Gardens to think about her task. It was early, her eyes were dazzled by the sunlight on the frost; tiny stars hit the pond and vanished under the water. She decided Isabella Raleigh should have a small tartan square.

In Nash's, Alice placed her thoughts, one by one, around the imagined head of Isabella Raleigh, in order to choose the tartan. She studied each pattern, how the lines laid across each other, blending imperceptibly here, treacherously there. She chose MacDonald of Boisdale, dress quality, ten ounce, and decided to buy the bare minimum of fabric. This would make it difficult to stretch the material into the shape, and there would be no room for mistakes—she would do penance for her bitterness. Clutching her roll of fabric, she moved away from the tartans towards the black velvets: that one, velveteen, or— She stroked the naps, considering their relative depth, sulkily. Once again she selected the smallest possible amount, an amount that would cause her suffering in the making.

She moved over to the black brocades and ribbons. These must not diminish the tartan, they must have angles rather than curves; the ribbon must be flat and not watermarked. Next, the lining: Alice must have only the purest satin for Madame's perfect head, only the purest black satin to lie over the purest curls. In fact, what Alice really wanted to do was to make a hat for suspicion—a tartan square for suspicion. Suspicion—rendered in the fact that there was slightly too little material, so that no error could occur in the making; present in the sharpness of the corners of the square, in the cut of the pom-pom placed precisely, to a millimetre, at the centre of the square. And all would be made secure with the tiniest of stitches.

*

Alice returned home to find that Dr. Firbank's analysis had, at last, arrived: she recognized the writing at once. She took up the envelope and dropped it into her wastepaper basket: simply to imagine the results, she decided, would do quite as well. The envelope lay on top of scraps of brown paper and loops of thread. She retrieved the envelope. She slid her finger under the flap, and eased what appeared to be several thin folded papers out of the envelope. She laid them, still folded, on her desk. In front of her were her largest scissors. She would cut the papers into thin strips. She would weave the papers that purported to describe her moral character, her temperament, her disposition—her very soul—into the crown of the tartan square that she was making for Mrs. Isabella Raleigh. Then the information *he* required would be right there on top of the head of his mistress and he would not know it.

Alice turned the papers over, tapped them on the table to line the pages up, tapped them again and then she took her scissors and cut through Firbank's tight, forward-slanting script. She scooped the strips of paper up and put them into a box. She lay down on her bed. She put the white muslin over her eyes and tried to clear her mind. She cried a little.

But Alice could not contain her desire to know. She wanted—after all—the knowledge that John Motton wanted. She tried for an hour to piece the narrow strips together, but the analysis remained unreadable. She cried again. It was just as she had predicted: she could be dissolved and reconstituted only by virtue of a Phrenologist's knowledge.

St. Peter's bell chimed midnight. She had finished it: she had woven Dr. Firbank's lacerated analysis of her character into the structure of Mrs. Isabella Raleigh's tartan square. It now lodged between the facings on the brocade rim, and the satin and tartan inside the crown. She had taken special care so that it could not be felt, although it remained possible that Isabella would sense it and develop an itch; or that the paper would disintegrate and lie imperceptibly on top of Isabella's crow-black hair; or that the hat would fly off, be run over by a hansom and its secret revealed. Ah, soon she would be mad, Alice Heapy. She knew: quite mad.

XV

Alice could not rise. Around her bed were Miss Linden's designs, folded brown paper and tissue paper with words and black lines on them. It was blue outside her window—it must have been Sunday, for the Laundry was not branding its black smoke on the clear sky. She could not rise. She was pupa, she was a wet sloth escaping from the flood. Miss Linden's designs were all around the bed and soon Miss Linden's designs would materialise and Alice would rise, she would rise so that she could transform these messages into hats, which would be worn by Miss Linden for the occasion of her Transfiguration.

There was a knock at Alice's door. It was Mrs. Peake. She had heard sobbing, she said. She was concerned, she said. Mrs. Peake spoke through the door; in a channel of two inches Alice could see the central column of the woman's face, her whole curious fleshy mouth trying to fit into that central channel. Soon, thought Alice, Mrs. Peake would be telling her neighbours and the other tenants that she had a madwoman within the house, that there were spirits, perhaps, that she had seen things move, heard wailing and sobbing, and she wonders if it is Alice.

Alice said, 'Mrs. Peake, come into the room. See for yourself, there is no-one sobbing. Look—only designs, black lines and words on brown paper, on tissue paper, on newspaper. Here are threads, see—a basket of threads: cinnamon, vermilion, eye-blue, scarlet bird—look, Mrs. Peake, look closely. Come in, Mrs. Peake, come and sit on the bed here, let me touch your hand. Let me feel the lines and movement of your fingers, let me trace the muscles in your hands. Let me hold you for a second, let me touch the folds of your skirt, the damp of your apron.'

Mrs. Peake did not enter the room. She quietly closed the door. Perhaps she could hear Alice speaking; perhaps she thought Alice was asleep. *Let me sleep, for sleep is indivisible. If there is crying, it is for the loss of that which is whole.*

Today Alice could not rise, for the quiet, clear sky asked that she lie here to receive it. She could not rise. She would wait here, patiently, in this tomb. She would wait here endlessly whilst John Motton needed only thirty-five minutes to complete his work from beginning to end, in which he started, he stopped, clicked and calculated, moving sombrely round his victim—for he wanted to classify and categorise and to separate all species, one from another. And what would he have when it was all done? What would he have except names and labels? Classification: it was the opposite of wholeness. The wholeness of all, thought Alice, which is what cathedrals and temples and the Taj Mahal were for, and what her hats were for.

If she stood on her chair by the window Alice could see figures creeping below. She watched the figures for some time; she liked to observe their different rhythms, it was restful, it contrasted with the coursing of her needle through fabric, it was peace from the incessant movements that her hands must make.

And then she decided: she would make no more hats. She would take no more measurements, she would make no more designs, would no longer complete her hats by working through the night. Because soon, on Tuesday at half past five, she would endure what she had so long resisted. There was no longer any need to resist, for she had lain on printed silk with Miss Thirsk; she had been examined by Dr. Firbank; she had cut his analysis into quarter-inch strips and placed them inside the structure of a tartan square.

She must deliver the tartan square. She must go at once to Holland Park Mansions to deliver the tartan square.

Alice carefully placed Mrs. Raleigh's tartan square amongst red satin and tissue paper in her best black velvet hatbox. She wrapped herself in black velvet. She went out into the cold clear blue sky and along the quiet streets. As she turned into the Grove she could hear the howling of the wild dogs. She could smell the pig farm. She clutched the hatbox to her chest as she walked.

She stood opposite Holland Park Mansions. She could see the door by which John Motton had once entered, and the patterned window. She set the hatbox down on the doorstep, the hatbox containing the tartan square for Suspicion, and walked quickly away, clutching her black cape to her breast, walking away from the tartan square and Isabella Raleigh—walking away from the last hat she would make, walking wherever her feet took her.

She could hear church bells, and she thought of her series of hats for Nuns and Nurses, half finished, never to be finished. The Sisters were walking in pairs further along the street. They were entering a church to their right, a church made of orange-red bricks, they were walking through a little courtyard and in through a low, arched door in the corner. Alice brought her cape across her mouth and turned into the courtyard, walked through the low door in the corner. The Sisters had moved behind a screen, she could hear their low voices. The air was dark and sharp with incense. She knelt down in the barely lit church, listening to the soothing murmur of the voices behind the screen.

XVI

Today Alice would have her head delineated by Mr. John Motton. She would wear her white muslin dress, as she had for Mrs. Zaphinov. For she was to be renewed; she was to be measured into new life. She would sit aglow in the panelled gloom, sprung with whiteness, and in the semi-dark the instruments would gleam, as they did for Dr. Firbank; the instruments themselves would give her new life. She would embrace them.

She was ready: her 'museum' was complete. She had placed all her unfinished hats in hatboxes; the boxes were labelled and set in tiers. She had classified them not by the seasons for which they were made, not by the grand passions such as Anger, Pride and Jealousy, not by their shape nor their dominant fabric. They were simply labelled with the name of their commissioner: Mrs. Zaphinov, Miss Thirsk, Mrs. Motton, Miss Alice Heapy. The hatboxes were arranged in a semi-circle, an arc facing the length of Alice's bed. They formed a kind of amphitheatre—it was as if each hatbox contained a member of the Greek Chorus; they spoke as One. But during the night, Alice imagined, each would emerge from its box and creep about the stage—this one sorrowful, that one contorted and strange, this one serene, with blue veins, that one wriggling and scarlet. Ah—but in the morning they would speak as One, because that was their purpose: to bring together, not to separate or disassemble. Their role was to unify; they each, singly, represented unification.

Alice studied the semi-circle: some of the hatboxes were made of maple, one had banana leaves woven into the lid, two had wide ribbons, another a broken leather handle and a rusty clasp. She speculated that there had never been hats in any of the boxes, that all her work had been a fantasy, designs drawn painstakingly in sand.

Today Alice would have her head delineated by Mr. John Motton. She was early. She waited in the park. The sun moved in and out of the clouds. She watched red squirrels in the trees, leaping from branch to branch.

As I arrive at the Motton's house this afternoon he will be there at the window, his form growing larger and more distinct as I climb up the steps to the door. I will hope he will appear at the front door when I ring the bell, but no—a maidservant with a large mole on her chin will arrive in the doorway. Without speaking she will usher me inside and along the narrow hall. As my eyes grow accustomed to the dark I will find I am heading towards a tall man, broad, in a brown wool jacket with a waistcoat, a watch-chain looped across dark brown buttons. He will be wearing a primrose silk cravat.

'Ah, Alice, you are early!'

John Motton is very pleased. He places his heavy arm around Alice's shoulder and steers her into his Room. He nudges her towards the chair opposite his walnut desk. He shuts the door. His best silver callipers have been wrested from their purple satin; they are already assembled; they gleam. John Motton begins at once.

'It must be your *Agreeableness* that has brought you here at last, my dear Alice. The faculty is situated to the right and left of the capacity to judge human nature, and in front of *Benevolence* and *Imitation*.'

He places his fingertips on the corresponding section, just above Alice's hairline.

'*Agreeableness*—it seems that you have this faculty in the fourth or fifth degree—it suggests that you're rather adaptable to the company you're in.'

He writes down some notes in his leather-bound book, he dips his pen in the ink, he writes with quick strokes.

142

It is nothing, this Reading.

'Now then: Human Nature.' He studies her, he feels to the left of her skull, smirks a little. 'Yes, I suspect you have a fair discernment of human nature, but you don't trust in your decisions, and justly so, for they are not always right, not always, are they, Alice?'

Alice sinks down into her chair, her back against the curved, upholstered velvet. Motton circles her, brushes against her: she feels the wool, the hard round pocket-watch against her neck, the silk of his cravat on her face. He circles her: she is a puppet, a toy in his hands, which are solid and certain. He places these hands on her skull, one hand on each side; she feels her head expanding into the shape that his hands make. He extends the callipers over her brow, adjusting the screw, making notes. He does not speak now, only assesses each section. He lingers, he presses on her temples; she can feel her cheekbones beneath them. His hands smell of soap, she notices his manicured nails. He places his hands at the base of her skull. He brings his hands up behind her ears, his fingers tracing the bone behind the ears. At each section he announces its corresponding name: *Destructiveness, Colour.*

'Yes, as I thought, your eyebrows are arched at the centre—I think you have *Colour* in the fifth or an even higher degree—an intuitive perception of the harmony in the arrangement of colours. And *Form...*'

He feels, measures, categorises, interprets. 'Yes, you have *Form*, too, in the sixth or seventh—it means that you can see at a glance whether a thing is plumb in the centre or in proportion. And also that you have a good memory for faces.'

Next, *Individuality.* Then *Mirthfulness.* He isn't very interested in Mirth. *It is nothing, this Reading. It has no significance.* John Motton writes quickly and keenly in his leather-bound book. There is a look of deep satisfaction on

143

his face, a bead of sweat waiting above his lip, a lock of black hair escaping from his oiled pate on to the temple. His breath is a little uneven. Alice thinks she can hear his heart beating inside the thick wool of his jacket.

Let this Reading be nothing.

Motton is getting near to *Secretiveness*. He moves more slowly now. His hands are warm. He feels again, he measures, he stares into Alice's face. She tastes iron in her mouth. He does not write now. He gazes at her. She feels a stirring, her body is warm too—against her will, her body is beginning to offer itself. A sound is emitted from between his lips and he turns away. She knows he is working backwards from the last to the first faculty, the first being that of *Amativeness*, the capacity for *love*, the one Alice estimated for herself, in her room, in November.

'Alice, you look a little unwell.'

Birds pretend they are injured so that they will not be attacked. I am injured.

'I have almost finished the Reading, only two or three more sections, Alice.' His voice is unusually low. 'Try to keep control until we have finished, Alice. Another ten minutes, my dear.'

She is enslaved. She has surrendered by sitting down on that chair. She surrendered when she bought the little blue book, when she attended Fowler's lecture. She surrendered when she first saw John Motton framed in his front window.

'No!' Alice springs out of the chair. *You will not have me!*

She makes towards the door. He is already there, across the doorway, placing his hands on her two shoulders, one hand now on her cheek.

'Alice, you have nothing to fear. *I have neither rack nor surgeon's knife.* Let me finish the reading. It will help you.'

He shunts her back to the chair. He is solicitous. He smiles at her, his moustache spreading, his teeth strong and wide, with the gap in the middle. He is measuring for *Combativeness*. No doubt Alice has it in the largest degree: good opposing power. Difficulties and opposition, he says, will cause her to make use of her mind and traits of character that would otherwise remain dormant. But Alice does not need this system of classification—she does not need it at all. She likes the feel of her ladies' hair, she likes the shape of their faces—she likes the beauty of variety. She likes the different colours and textures of their skin because each one is unique and strange and has no explanation. She could seek a reason, say it was their blood, their ancestry—but what would she then know? If there was a reason, she did not need to know it.

Motton is getting close. He has almost finished, and Alice has kept her secrets. At the very moment of this thought, her cheeks burn, and one of her secrets is spilled.

'Forgive me, Sir—I have already submitted to analysis.'

Motton puts his leather book down on the desk.

'It was at Farringdon, Sir.'

He places his pen on top of his leather book. He walks over to the window, stares out through the glass pane.

'I am not so easily fooled, Miss Heapy. I know this is just another of your little tricks.' He turns round, leans down towards her face.

But Alice is invincible now: the first revelations, the ones he so desired, are woven into the hat of his mistress; they lie in a black velvet box on her doorstep.

'Now that you have had your little game, perhaps you would let me finish.'

She lets him finish. *Concentrativeness. Comparison. Causality. Amativeness.*

She lets him finish because he cannot know from numbers and inches what the human mind is capable of. She, Alice Heapy, would show him what the mind is capable of. She would be vague and incoherent; she would sing unmeaning verses to a terrible tune, over and over. She would no longer recognize him, nor her hat ladies, nor her own brother. She would not recognize herself. If anyone asked her a question she would answer with a single, unconnected word. Turnip, she would say on being asked if she was quite well; or red, or scarlet or carmine, cardinal, crimson, magenta or cerise, depending on the time of day. She would scream and tear at her clothing, lurch towards the window, whisper prayers, the entire Sacrament, then set to her singing once again. She would sing the song of Prince Albert, a poisoner's song. She would rush upon John Motton, she would climb him, placing one foot here, another there. She would visit him in the early afternoon; she would rush into the hallway, pushing Mary aside, and burst into the Consulting Room during one of his Readings.

'Professor!' she would shriek, 'Professor, I am the God of Air!' And she would hurtle towards the window and pull violently at the velvet drapes. 'Allow me to help you, madam' he would say in a voice waxy with anger and disgust, and he would put his arms over her chest and hurl her away, out into hallway and on to the steps. Then she would become calm, as if full of shame, and weep a little.

Yet she lets him finish, for his analysis transformed Miss Linden—his analysis has transfigured a woman.

'I shall send you the results in due course, Miss Heapy.' He is ushering her out of the Room, away from the ventilating hat and the globe and the porcelain head, past the humming bird in its glass case, past the collection of ivory ladies' legs, out of the Room into the hallway and on to the street.

Back in her room, Alice lit a candle and assembled her pens and inks and paper. She sat down at her table and wrote letters to Mrs. Zaphinov, Miss Linden, Mrs. Motton, and Miss Thirsk. She would leave the letters in the last hatbox on the right of the arc, with the Hat for Black Grace, which must not be worn.

To Mrs. Zaphinov she wrote:

'The hats I could not finish for you are in the hatboxes marked with your name: a series, a procession, in brilliant colours and embroidered with clouds and sunrays. They are made to be unfinished, like you, Mrs. Zaphinov, who must spill and froth.'

To Miss Linden:

'I dreamt that you and Mr. Motton were once betrothed—and now you are, in the way he has transformed you. Your hats, the Taj Mahal and the Tent Series and the Parting Fish, are in the boxes marked with your name.'

To Mrs. Motton:

'I have placed your hats on the bottom row at the front, so that you can reach them. I have curled all the feathers.'

Her letter to Miss Thirsk:

'Your hats are in the boxes in the centre of the arc. They are the most beautiful of all.'

And Edward:

'I have tried looking in mirrors, in water, in silver. Not for a reflection but for an essence. I am not looking for definition, as John Motton is, but the opposite of definition. Indeed, you might argue that I should not 'look' at all, that I need only exist for knowledge to avail itself, in the ways it knows best: secret, silent ways.'

Tomorrow she would also write a letter to Mrs. Isabella Raleigh, and one for John Motton.

She had letters for John Motton and Isabella. It was three o'clock in the afternoon. Alice walked up and down outside Motton's window, dragging one foot behind her. At half past three Mary came out on the top step and stared at Alice with her arms folded. Alice refused to catch Mary's eye, instead began her singing, then, just as Mary turned to go back into the house Alice rushed up the steps and caught her elbow.

'I know you.' Alice hissed. 'I know you.' Mary wrenched herself away and shut the door against Alice's shoulder.

She had a letter for John Motton, but first she would show him how a mind worked, what the human mind is capable of. She would show him that the mind is as complex as a glass of water: still, with a layer of bubbles clinging to the side of the glass; that it moves at the slightest drift of air; it moves when the sun shines on it, when the light alters with the passing of a cloud or a bird. It is pure, transparent; kind as breath. It reflects, it covers, it lays smooth across any surface. It creates new light, rainbows and concentric circles of blues and violets. It draws light towards itself. It gives, it absorbs, which is its special work. It hears voices that are low and still, telling of others, telling secrets of others. Tell Alice nothing. Let the mind tell her nothing. Ah, singing, the mind is singing, let the mind call like birds, like swallows above the air, high, high; or the bark-croak of a pheasant; or a human cough. The mind is as innocent as water, and capable at once of drowning a woman, of calling a woman down.

And she knew that John Motton was frightened of the mind, that he was frightened of his own mind. That it played tricks on him, made him suffer in the rooms of Mrs. Isabella Raleigh. That it had brought him to a profession not of his choosing, it made him in thrall to his mother. She imagined his mind to be laden; full with sand, ochre-red clay, cut through with threads and fissures. That John Motton's mind was opaque, it was not a glass of water; his mind was his brain, his cerebrum, a lightly pleated mass beneath his skull. And with every measurement, with every client, every pen-mark detailing inches and pattern, this smooth, wet mass diminished, until he would surely have the brain of an imbecile, or a woman. Delineate, demarcate, line, angle and number: this was not love, it was barely even mind. It was his elbow or his shinbone working, his long cold shinbone, where his mind should be.

Alice had a hat for John Motton. It was colourful and strong. It was made from fruit and flies and leaves, a bird's beak, a shell, a gem, a mirror and the prayer she had said for Miss Thirsk's bird. It had built itself. It was constantly changing, mutating, it was Evolution embodied: matter, fossil, crystal. It lived. It changed. John Motton must wear Evolution on his head. He would cry, she would see great drops of pale fluid easing out from behind his eyes, the miracle of tears. Let all minds cry; or let the brain laugh, to create space between itself and the skull. Let the mind be the space between the skull and matter, the space created by mirth. Mirth, the origin of mind.

He had said once, 'Alice'—he used to call her Alice then—'Of course, my dear (*my silly dear*), what we Phrenologists are dealing with are Propensities, not the actual things in themselves. For example, there is no such thing as Love, only the capacity, the *propensity* to love. That is to say, one cannot measure Love, only a tendency towards Conjugality; only predict the propensity to marry and live successfully with a member of the other sex. So, we do not talk of Love, but only of that which is explicable by recourse to method.'

Alice knocked at the door. No one came. She leant over the railings and knocked on John Motton's window. He appeared behind the glass; she could see another head, with dark curls. She called out, 'I have a method, Sir: I sing. I hear my mind singing, it moves, its movement is the same thing as love. Trace the line. It is barely a line, rather a whisper—you see, you cannot touch it and yet it is there. It sings, it breathes, it sings a loose song—here, try it, Sir. Here, take this glove—I made it myself. It is cinnamon kid, three buttons to the side. Let the fingers flap near your eyes—this way, that way—let your nose relax, Sir. Relax, Sir. You see, I can mesmerize you with the loose fingers of my cinnamon kid glove. Look how your eyes swivel and switch. Try it yourself Sir, sing—*sing*,' she shouted. 'Here, Sir: we shall dance whilst you sing. I already have you, my hand on your hand, up above our shoulders, my other hand pressed against your shoulder. I love you. If you were a flea or a snail or an inanimate object I should love you. I wanted you to love me once; but I have love enough—it circles me, occasionally it lands, and I inspect it with the magnifying glass, the one I stole from your desk.

'Give me your hand, Sir, lay your fingers here, and here, for Love's sake, not for me, but for Love. See, it is warm, it receives you. Show me *your* heart, John Motton: show me where it connects to the rest of your body. I must see your heart, Sir, let us measure it. Let this be the day we measure John Motton's heart. Ah, Sir—it is exactly the size of your brain, Sir, with a protrusion here, a visibly-beating propensity there. Try to relax, Sir. I am only measuring your heart, and I try to have no *Judgement*, I try to have no propensity for *Judgement*. I measure, but I throw away my results.

'But Sir: you have indeed a little love for Isabella! She is there with you now, I can see her. And of course I have seen you when she has visited, I have followed you to her rooms in Holland Park, and I have seen you afterwards; you walked differently on the way home.'

You are a sorceress, girl, spying on me. Try to mind your own business, get on with my mother's spring hat. I want you to finish my mother's spring hat, in the colour she wants it, nesting in a silk box with a beautiful red ribbon.

'You see, he loves: he wants a red ribbon: he loves. He strikes love every time he says the word 'beautiful', every time he laughs at his mother's little ways, every time he fetches her gloves.'

John Motton suddenly opened the door.

You! You sorceress, stop it! Stop. You think you have knowledge about me, but you know nothing. You meddle, you pry; you wish to strip me to the bone. Go!

'Miss Heapy. Kindly go home or I shall call a policeman.' He shut the door.

Behind Alice's eyes was a redness, a gold light. It was quiet there, the redness covered the inside of the forehead; now it was green, black, striped across in yellow. It was the division and rearrangement of a whole into sections and parts, the dissection of that which is indivisible.

Alice began once again to walk up and down beneath Motton's window, dragging one foot behind her. She could see him at the window once more; she could see he was chewing something. Again she rushed up the steps. 'I have a letter for you, Sir. I have a letter for you.'

XVII

John Motton was walking from Kensington to Farringdon. He leant forward, taking large strides against a cold wind. His whiskers flew back, his cheeks were scorched. His coat flapped and this annoyed him. He would throw a brick at the windows of Fowler's Institute at Ludgate Circus. Usurpers! Perhaps he would find a brick lying on the ground. A fine British tradition of careful scientific view and review, usurped by an American with a clownish beard. And damned Firbank: he would wring the man's neck. He had been—*cuckolded*.

He banged on a door. The paint was black and worn, there were leaves at the single stone step. Dr. Firbank opened the door a little. Motton could see a strip of purple coat and white ruff. Motton pressed his foot into the narrow gap. Dr. Firbank did not appear to recognize him. He brought his face close up to the old man, who drew back, hissing: 'What devil has brought you here? Be gone with you, man!'

John Motton eased his shoulder against the door. 'I just want the answer to two simple questions, Sir. First, have you recently delineated a young woman—Miss Alice Heapy, a milliner—and second, have you joined that— Fowler Institute?'

'And what business is it of yours? I do not discuss clients, Sir, neither my professional circumstances.' Firbank tried to close the door. 'Good day to you, Sir.'

The violence of John Motton was great—he shoved open the door, causing the old man to stumble backwards.

'How dare you, Sir...'

John Motton marched straight through a door off the hallway—a desk, a mirror, an empty grate—books, dust, an old wooden trolley piled with papers and books. John picked up one of the books: Pepys, the Bible. Another, another—no Charts, no Combe, no Spurzheim.

'Where do you keep it all?' he shouted.

Firbank leant against the doorframe, trembling. 'You young ruffian.'

John Motton turned, suddenly calm. He held out his hand, which Firbank gingerly accepted. 'John Motton.'

'I know exactly you who are,' said the old man.

John looked away, then, 'Are you still practicing? Has Fowler got you?'

'Fowler has indeed revived an interest in the science, Sir. I have had business since they started up. By the end of the fifties I was almost ruined. You will have benefitted too, of course.'

Motton swung towards the old man. 'Yes, Firbank, the *science*. Fowler has thrown it all away. He invites any young fool artisan or engineer to start up. How can you agree with *that?*'

'Are you or I any better than an artisan or an engineer, Sir? What skills do you possess other than those of Phrenology? Could you help to design a bridge or a railway? Could you tailor a suit?'

'Oh shut up, man—whose side are you on, for God's sake? Ach! Just tell me, did you see that young milliner, two weeks, two months ago? Alice Heapy. Miss Alice Heapy.'

'I cannot remember names, Sir—I've done twenty-five delineations in a fortnight—however many in two months. You're asking too much of me, Sir.'

John Motton looked at the old man's scrawny neck, made yet more scrawny by his stiff ruff. 'How did you know my father? Did you train together? I don't believe I met you at Kensington; perhaps it was at the London Institute.'

'Your father and I met on a number of occasions to discuss Combe and how we could accommodate

153

Spurzheim's ideas; and not long before he died, he came to me for some, shall we say, *professional* advice.'

John Motton loosened his cravat. Firbank knew something. And he remembered Alice Heapy; he remembered her all right.

'Look, sir, I apologise for my rudeness. Let me buy you a whisky, Sir. Come, let me take you to my Club—we'll hail a cab and pitch up with a whisky at my Club.'

On the way to Jackson's Club for the Science and Medical Professions, John Motton thought to soften the old man by disclosing a few personal details.

'He used to practise on me, my father, measured me every three months as I was growing—it seemed that he was measuring me every day, as if trying to will certain Faculties to develop.'

Firbank looked straight ahead. Perhaps he was a bit deaf; John Motton began to talk more loudly. Firbank flinched at the increased volume. Motton went on—'I'll tell *you* this, in confidence, Sir—I didn't measure up. I didn't damn well measure up!' John Motton glimpsed his face in the carriage window.

They arrived at the Club. Motton helped the old man out of the carriage, up the steps into the Club. He was greeted by the doorman and the porter and the clerk at Reception, and the two sat down in deep hard green leather chairs. They were opposite one another, next to a roaring fire. A waiter appeared, disappeared and reappeared with two large measures of whisky in cut glass tumblers. Firbank cradled his glass with his bony hands.

'She's small,' began Motton, 'about five foot two, curly hair, brown—light brown, fair, even—do you know, I can't even remember. Sorceress—wicked. An air of mischief about her. Green eyes. A little witch.'

Firbank closed his eyes as if trying to remember. He seemed to be taking immense pleasure in swirling the whisky around his old cheeks, as if he were letting the liquor penetrate his gums and his throat. He kept his eyes closed.

'Here, have another. Waiter! Now come on you old goat—you must remember her—you don't get the likes of her every day.'

Firbank lifted the second glass to his loose wet lips.

'Actually I do,' said Firbank, finally opening his eyes. 'I do get the likes of those feisty little milliners every single day coming along to know themselves. Instead of going to church, these little lasses come to me and have me shake my great wobbly hands over their heads and then they fall down yelping and demanding absolution: I feel like Jesus Christ Himself after a week of them.'

John Motton grimaced. Thank goodness this stream of milliners was flowing out to Farringdon and not to Kensington—it must be, he realised, on account of Firbank's proximity to the infernal Fowler Institute at Ludgate.

Firbank finished his whisky. 'Why are you so concerned over this milliner, Sir?' he asked, very carefully placing his empty glass on the table between the two men.

'She's ill, Firbank—an acute mental condition, probably monomania. It came on recently. She's my mother's milliner—a very fine little hat maker indeed, in fact. The illness may have developed after she visited you, and I—wondered if you could throw any light on—do you have her results?'

'Oh no, I always post the results—they're perfectly self-explanatory, these new charts. And I never keep a copy. Clutter.'

Motton took a slug of whisky. 'You remember her, don't you?'

155

'You know, Sir, your father was very involved in helping to treat cases of monomania at the restored Bethlem—actually, first of all at Wakefield. He was a very eminent man in his field, your father. Highly respected. Handsome man, too. How's that dear wife of his—your mother, of course?'

'She's as she ever was, nervous, demanding. She frets. You know what they're like.'

'Actually, Sir, I am a bachelor. My mother has been dead for fifty years. I have no sisters. I do not, in fact, know what 'they' are like, except through my work. Indeed, I'm surprised you've come to me to discuss a case of monomania when you've had the expertise in your own family.'

Motton would have blushed if he had been capable of doing so, for it seemed suddenly that he knew less about monomania or any mental disease than this wretched milliner who was either a talented, nay, brilliant, actress, or she was indeed *en route* to Bethlem. He leant forward. Firbank leant forward, too, tipping his empty glass towards the younger man.

'Look, Firbank, she's a very unusual young woman—a very interesting specimen. I had wanted the privilege of examining her for six months—indeed, between you and me I was wooing her, as it were, trying to persuade her to agree to a delineation. She expressed a distinct interest in the profession, in fact she seems to know a great deal about it, and—as I say—I had looked forward to the honour of examining her myself.

'However,' Motton stiffened, 'whilst I was in the process of analysing her, she declared that she had already visited a Phrenologist: your good self, Sir.'

Firbank brushed his fingers lightly along the side of his empty glass. Motton summoned the waiter once again. Two more glasses of the chestnut liquor were set down between the two men. The fire flickered. Firbank leant back in his green leather, his voluminous purple coat bunched up at one side. Now he spread it out fussily, over the arms of the chair and around his legs.

'She is a sorceress,' continued Motton, 'such that I hardly believed her when she said she had already been delineated. It would be quite in character—she has gross *Secretiveness*, and a highly developed *Imitativeness*. Damn it! She was always spying on me, following me. She seems to have made it her life's mission to interfere with my daily business since she first came to work for my mother. I tried to keep her away, when Mother was a little unwell; and I have several times suggested to Mother that she already has quite enough hats. The woman is poisoning us!'

'That's a very strong word, "poisoning",' said Firbank. 'My recollection of the little lass was of a kind of intense purity, a dark purity, if such a thing could exist. *But ah—this whisky—luscious, Scottish whisky*—but then, perhaps I am thinking of the wrong lass.'

John Motton felt like kicking the man. He seemed to be keeping each slurp of whisky in his mouth as long as possible before swallowing. He was surely smirking. John Motton stood up, glaring down Firbank, who now looked a little abashed. 'So, come on, old man—what was it that my father consulted you about? Tell me. Or I'll make a scene.'

Firbank straightened up. 'Now now, Sir—a scene! Why, you have no idea how *little* I have to lose by your making a 'scene'. Surely you know that I sold my soul to Fowler five years ago, in 1860. I was—a breath—a breath away from the workhouse. I am certainly not going to be threatened now by an ignorant bully like you.' He tried to pull himself up, but his coat trapped him, and he simply tipped back his head.

Motton repeated, 'What was it that my father consulted you about? What was it?'

'You, Sir, and—' Firbank hesitated, 'and a female client.'

'He consulted *you* about *me?*'

'Yes, Sir. Your father was a little concerned at one time —nothing other than a father's natural concern for the— *direction* his son might take.'

'And the woman, Firbank, the woman?'

'Ah, now that detail I cannot remember, Sir—I seem not to have a head for remembering women. They all seem alike to me.'

'I'm a bachelor myself,' cried Motton, 'and they all seem completely distinct to me!'

He thought of how he focused on the minute differences between women, the way some wore their sleeves right down on their hands and others rolled them back; their hands, the shape and length of their fingers. He noticed, of course, their foreheads, temples, their cerebella—if pronounced they were likely to be little hussies. He liked looking at the little place just above their lips, at their noses when they spoke. And at the way their legs moved beneath their skirts, under their skirts. He could look at their legs, concealed, or revealed, all night long.

'Anyway, man, look at this letter. It's from her, the milliner. I believe she is threatening suicide. Would you, with your professional experience, conclude that we're dealing with a case of monomania? It would help if you could, Sir.'

Firbank received the letter into his shaking hands. The script was small and even.

Dear John Motton,

A life is only a procession of small movements and sounds towards its end. But you are not interested in life, only in 'character'. You don't have a theory for the minute and painful business of living. Now that you have made your Reading, you imagine that you know me, the whole of me, each breath I have taken. You imagine you can know me

158

by the formation of my bone structure in one small part of my body. And thus you have cut my life short, for I cannot live whilst I am judged. I cannot con tort to satisfy a scientific theory; I cannot satisfy you, whether I am different or the same. I cannot satisfy you.

Improvement—for what? How will I know if I have been successful if I take your advice? What special shape should I make that you would approve of me? I cannot improve my class or my degree of conjugality by the method of your profession.

Yet I wanted you to describe me. I wanted to be known—although I have learnt to know myself by the shapes I have made and by the colours I have selected, in the discoveries I have made in the comparison of silk and tulle; in the recognition of my professional mistakes. I have inquired into the lies I have told; I have studied my habits. As for my 'character', it is but your invention. I do not answer to its call.

If character is important at all it cannot be delineated by measuring bumps and organs: it takes a whole life to its end to reveal someone's nature.

Thus I wear the Hat of Black Grace: wearing it I may meet death as an equal.
Alice Heapy,
Milliner

Firbank coughed a little and laid the letter down on the table. He closed his eyes. John Motton waited. Perhaps he was going to consider the matter with his eyes closed. He kicked Firbank's ankle. The old man sucked in breath. He picked up the letter.

'She seems most—rational, Sir, until that last line about the Hat of Black Grace. I rather agree with her.' He laughed.

John Motton stood up. He towered over the man: the thin, purple man who had become foolish with liquor, sitting in a green chair lit by the flicker of orange flames: an old Phrenologist who had sold his soul—and John Motton

159

was striding out of the Lounge and down the steps of Jackson's Club.

John Motton asked the carriage driver to put him down near Battersea Park. He had heard there were women there who would give him some relief. He would at last, after all, allow himself a little relief.

He stood for a while under a gas lamp near the Bridge, blowing on his hands, feeling the money in his pocket. Then he walked down towards the Park gates. On the promenade was a throng of young men and women; a brass band was playing; further along, a thick circle of people roared and clapped at something Motton couldn't see. Two or three women walked up and down near the hedge. John Motton watched one of them for a few minutes: she was short, buxom; he liked her stoutness. He felt in his pockets for his money, and then he couldn't see the little wench any more. He cast around for her, and his eye alighted on a painted sign over a booth by the park gates: '*Phrenology*'.

John Motton stood very still. He stared at the sign. Outside the booth was a queue of people: the *working classes, artisans!* A young man was coming out through a red curtain, he was chuckling to himself. John Motton stepped forward and joined the queue. He waited in the cold, rubbing his hands, registering the faces of each of the young men and women as they came out of the booth. He was next in line. He was no longer cold. His hands were clammy now. He took some snuff. His hands were trembling a little. He was stepping towards the booth, he was in the booth.

He stood opposite the Phrenologist, a man looking like Santa Claus with a white beard and curly white hair. He stood opposite the Phrenologist, and John Motton now saw that the man had rouged cheeks and that his white hair was a wig. He stood opposite the—rouged man, and suddenly he couldn't catch his breath, and the Phrenologist was asking for a guinea, one guinea, Sir, for the Reading. Motton tore a guinea from his pocket and threw it down—stumbling out through the curtain, out of the booth, on to the promenade. He doubled over by the hedge, to be sick.

XVIII

Motton climbed the stairs. He scuffed each one with his leather shoe. He disturbed a stone and a ball of dust. He climbed slowly, in the darkness of the stairwell, as if these steps would not end and he should pace himself. He was bringing the notes from Alice's Reading, and her little chart, and the letter she had written to him.

He climbed these stairs behind the bustling skirts of Alice's landlady. She greeted him at the door before he had even knocked, and she gave him the coy smile of someone who especially liked to be in the presence of a gentleman. No doubt she had *Alimentiveness, Approbation* and *Amativeness* each in the fifth degree, a competitive, grubbing little woman who yet had a warm heart. She turned frequently to see that Motton was keeping up with her, and to have another look at him, to offer another coquettish smile.

It was taking long to get up this staircase: they arrived at a landing, they paused, but Mrs. Peake did not knock on either of the doors; they paused again, and set off up another flight. The steps were narrower this time. His body was lead-heavy; the two proceeded increasingly slowly, as if the purpose of their scaling this ascent was the ascent itself, as if no single step would take them any higher. They reached the next and final landing. There was one door, a low narrow door, tongue and groove; there were grease marks round its handle. This was the door to the place where Alice Heapy stitched and steamed, made deft movements with her small, muscular fingers.

The woman rapped cleanly on the door; the wood soaked up the impact. She rapped again, moving her shoulder towards the door, putting her mouth up to the crack between the door and its frame.

'Miss Heapy! Gen'leman to see you! The physician!'

There was no reply. John Motton's heart beat beneath its jacket and waistcoat and shirt.

'Miss Heapy!' Mrs.Peake rapped more loudly. 'She may be asleep, Sir, I expect she's asleep, I'm certain she hasn't gone out—I always know when they're in or out, my people. I have my master key—let us enter.'

She fumbled at the lock and the latch and prised open the door. Alice was there, sitting on a chair, leaning forward a little. She was still wearing the white garments she had worn for the Reading two days before. She looked up. Her face glowed white. The window was open. No fire or candle drew the room this way or that. The bed was tightly made, the pillow plumped; everything in order. There was a semi-circle of hat boxes, a crescent, along one wall. There were no threads or scraps of material, no scissors or pins, nothing to suggest the life of a milliner except the closed hatboxes.

'I'll leave you two in peace, then, thank you very much, Sir.'

Motton had the feeling the wretched woman was waiting for a tip.

'Thank you, Madam. I can let myself out.'

She shut the door behind her. Alice was staring into the middle distance, both her hands now clasped in her lap.

'Do not tell me, Sir.'

She said it so simply that Motton would have wept if he was not a gentleman and an eminent Phrenologist.

'Why not, Alice? It is only what you know.'

'Then you do not need to tell me, Sir.'

'It will help you, Alice—it will give you the confidence of Science to bolster your intuitive knowledge.'

'I have no need of the confidence of Science, Sir.'

'Everyone needs that, Alice, now that it is possible.'

'Do not tell me, Sir.'

163

'You are something of a tease, then, Alice—'

She looked up at him. 'No, Sir.'

'You make me a little cross, Miss Heapy—I am a busy, professional man.'

'Yes, Sir.'

'Did you not think you wanted what I had to teach you, when you agreed to analysis?'

'You can teach me nothing, Sir.'

'Now Miss Heapy, that is rather disrespectful, is it not?'

'Perhaps, Sir, but it is the truth.'

'Surely you know that the truth is not always what is required, nor even necessary.'

'I do not know that, Sir.'

Motton moved nearer to her.

'Please do not come towards me, Sir.'

'Why ever not? You have had me close to you many times before.'

'Not now, though, Sir—'

'Is it because we are alone in your room?'

'No, Sir.'

'Do you fear that I may try to seduce you, Alice?'

It was pleasurable to him, this game. She looked up at him again.

'No Sir, it would be impossible.'

'Would it, Alice?' He moved a fraction nearer to her. She remained as if glued to her chair.

'Yes, Sir.' She looked down again.

Motton retreated a little, to test the effect. *Teasing hussy.* He moved to the open window.

'Bishop's Laundry. Is that what I can smell?'

'I expect so, Sir.'

He looked at her again. He decided she was no less sane than he was. 'And why did you agree to allow me in at all?'

'I did not, Sir, Mrs. Peake opened the door and showed you inside, saying you were the physician.'

'Where are all your milliner's tools, your fabrics? I was hoping to see the milliner at work—amidst all her taffeta and gleaming instruments.'

For some reason an image of the booth at Battersea Park came into his mind.

'I have disposed of them, Sir.'

'Where?'

The rouged cheeks, the wig that came too low over the forehead.

'Of what concern is it to you?'

'I am employing you, am I not? My mother's order, for which you have received an advance for materials, has not been received.'

'Her hats and designs are in those boxes, there, marked with Mrs. Motton's name. You can take them with you now.'

'Are you ceasing to practise as a milliner, then, Miss Heapy?'

'Yes, Sir.'

'And how will you live?'

She did not answer. The room felt very cold.

'Shall I close the window, Alice? Aren't you cold?'

'No, Sir.'

'Yes you are. I can see the tip of your nose is pink.'

Motton moved towards her, behind her. 'Let me warm you.'

He moved closer, expecting her to rise from her seat. She did not. He thought of the little wench with the stocky legs. He sniffed. He touched Alice's shoulder with his fingers. He laid the palm of his hand on the back of her neck, moving his fingers across the top vertebrae of her spine.

'Sir!'

The protest, he decided, was desultory.

'It is what you always desired, Alice, all these months.'

165

'I do not desire it now, Mr. Motton, Sir.'

He moved round to face her. He placed his fingers under her chin. 'I don't believe you, my dear. I can feel the warmth of your feelings beneath my fingertips.'

'I do not have any feelings, Sir.'

'Everyone has feelings, Alice Heapy, especially you. It is what your Reading shows most strongly.'

'You are wrong, Sir.'

Still she did not move. He wondered if she was indeed frozen to her chair. He decided to retreat a little. He studied the crescent of hatboxes.

'Show me what's inside those boxes, Alice—for I suspect they are empty.'

'You can take the boxes I showed you with your mother's hats and designs inside, Sir.'

'I want to see inside the other boxes.'

'I will not show you, Sir.'

'Why ever not? Will it spoil your artistic arrangement?'

'It will spoil something, Sir.'

'And what is that, Madam?'

'It will spoil my life.'

'Really Alice, so melodramatic.'

'It is the truth.'

'Hmmm, that again. The truth is nothing, Alice, you have set far too much store by it. It is your class, your artisan class—you all want the Truth. Hah! Truth!'

'You are the Devil to speak so, Sir. And you a Scientist!

'Yes, but more amusing, don't you agree, than the piety that you are currently exhibiting? I suppose you have forsaken millinery in order to take your vows?'

She did not reply. He would press her now. He snatched up her hand and pulled her off the chair and towards the bed. At first she was limp, passive. Perhaps she is a virgin, he thought. He could not tell from her blushes or her later struggling whether she was or not. In a sense, it made no difference: she was an innocent, a bloodless innocent. He decided she was indeed a virgin. His desire peaked and waned at once. Something like compassion now lay in his chest. Something he had not felt for a long while, something he may not have experienced before.

She began to cry, a sad, soft weeping.

Motton walked out on to the landing. He had one foot hovering, he was going to go down the stairs quickly, but he lingered. One of his gloves had fallen by the doorframe. He moved back towards the door. His hand rested on the latch. He went back into Alice's room.

Alice heard Mrs. Peake calling. Mrs. Peake was calling and padding up the stairs. She was knocking at the door in the way she always knocked. Her fist was formed, her fat fingers were tucked into her palm, and her dimpled knuckles were making contact with the door: rap, rap. Quiet. Now her name, whispered, 'Miss Alice'. Alice heard the ss's—Miss Aliss. Rap. Mrs. Peake was trying to enter, hooking the black latch up and over. It was too loud. Hush. She had lifted up the latch: she was inside.

'Miss Heapy, lass, what are you doing? The death of us —let me close that window.' She leant over to pull the window tight towards her, the glass at her bosom, a glass bosom, her breath on the window pane; she was twitching and fussing.

'Look at you. White as chalk, and not a blanket in sight. Where's your blanket?' Alice had no blanket. She had cut it up, she had unravelled it, put strips of it into Miss Thirsk's travelling hat.

'What have you done with it? A good blanket that was, I keep one for all my people. Where's your coat? Let me put your coat round your shoulders, Miss, let me fetch the physician—no, I'm sure we can manage. I shall get you some hot water. Let me just put this coat around your shoulders.'

Alice was small as a child as Mrs. Peake put the coat round her shoulders. She had lost years, all her adult years; her mother could put a coat around her shoulders. Hush. She kept her eyes closed; her lips felt small, innocent as a child's: little threads and lines, the seamless join of two types of skin. Perfection. Eye: see how it moves, how it flickers. Eye: revealing the world: open, shut, open, shut; the game of the eye. How it must laugh. *Mirthfulness*. Miss Thirsk had it. She was so prettily, so deliciously *sly*. Sly must be part of *Mirthfulness*. Where was it located now? It must be behind the eyes—ah, there it is, coolly waiting, waiting and sly, untouched by other organs.

Mrs. Peake was whispering, 'Dear Love, dear oh dearie me, dear Lord, you're frozen to the marrow. Look at that— no fire in the grate. Not a speck of coal. And to think I never noticed before, lassie, I'm a bad'un, that's what. Rock-a-bye, rock-a-bye—ah, my dear.'

The mind, Alice knew, has fronds; they skim the surface of the water, skim the surface of a reflection; fronds that shimmer above flat water. They alter according to the seasons, to the changes in light. John Motton could not see the changes in light, even though that is all there is in the world: very minute changes in light. Shade, dark, shadow, grey: colour only by virtue of light. Form, grain, texture: all made by light. Depth, surface, flat, round, concave, convex: all for light. Listen to birdsong, hear the pitch change with the changing light. Trill, coo, twist, roll, repeat, high trill; like the mind, a lace of sounds.

Mrs. Peake's hand had uncoiled, it was placing itself damply on Alice's forehead, the plump pads beneath each of her finger joints, the pad below the base of her thumb, all were now placed damply on Alice's forehead, now on her cheek. Her cheek drew itself towards Mrs. Peake's

plump padded hand, drew itself towards the dampness—
Alice's face between the warmth of Mrs. Peake's two damp
hands.

Alice was stilled, silent; she listened to the birds outside
the window, and to Mrs. Peake's powdery breathing—and
her pink face full and dropping down above Alice, her eyes
tiny humbugs popping between her cheeks and her brows.
She was held in Mrs. Peake's arms. Mrs. Peake was holding
Alice.

*'But I required that hat by Tuesday. This is really too distressing.
Yes, the one with the goose feathers over the eyes—for an important
occasion, with the Moy-Esgar-Moys. What, Miss Heapy, am I to do
now?'*

*'Of course, she always refused to use straw, you know, because of
her poor mother, because of her poor dear mother.'*

'She had things I wanted. She had what I wanted.'

*'You could never have satisfied him, Miss Heapy. He likes me,
in red and black lace, sometimes in white lace. He likes to turn me
this way and that. This way, and that.'*

*'She refused to operate by the rules, that little milliner. An
egotistical girl, always drawing attention to herself. Her death will be,
no doubt, a little more of her showing off.'*

Mrs. Peake was singing now. She was singing a lullaby.
God, let her sing, thought Alice, for she moves the light
with her song. 'I shall call back the physician at once, my
dear,' she said, and resumed her singing.

Someone was running their fingertips very lightly over
Alice's face. The fingers were on her lips now, trying to
ease them apart, to feel the flesh on the inside. When that
was done, there was quiet. Earlier it was so noisy —she was
under the little table there, her body was twitching, strange
little jerks of the limbs; she had to keep her head covered,
and to make herself as small as possible. Something was
playing a trick on her, her limbs jerking about for no reason

at all, they were moving quite uninvited. After that she was in the bed, covered over with the sheet, right at the bottom of the bed—sometimes the island was near—sometimes far—all depended upon the light—no air, still twitching—and there were voices, people trying to help, making suggestions, insisting she must choose. Then she was sitting upright with her head against the white wall and her mind, her brain, the space between her skull and matter, was being sucked from the back of her head. The wall was taking her mind, sucking it out. It was madness; madness wanted her. It had beckoned her before, tried to lure her behind, or inside, the wall. What place was that? Somewhere with more light, or less, or a place where there is no recognition of changes in the light.

He was tweed, coarse; he wore hard shoes with stitches like ants marching. They smashed across her boards, making her patterns rustle, making her hat boxes tremble. And that was not enough for him—he turned, his mustard-glazed face came back at her, she was minute before him. She wished for invisibility, for camouflage, the strike of a match to distract him—but he continued to approach. Sssh. Sssh. The coarse tweed was on her arms, his whole body was on her body, the tweed was scratching her arms, the mustard-glaze was dripping on to her face, he covered her bare lips with his whiskered lips, he was grazing her, he was squashing her lips, they were no longer lips; her eyes no longer eyes. He was moving with a kind of rhythm, almost a rhythm, something repeated yet undefined, he was moving in this almost rhythm and she was moving slightly along and back, along, and back, with the force of his almost rhythm. His lips continued to crush hers but this was not a kiss. Then there was a sound. At first she did not know where it was coming from; an animal sound. It was a growl, coming from underneath, a growl rising, becoming higher, higher, then it was in her mouth, distorting her mouth, the animal sound was between his mouth and hers, the sound that seemed not to belong to her. And Mrs. Peake was rapping at the door, and he was upright, calm as wood. The sound in her body rose up, independent of her mind, which was slipping, nearly slipping out through the white wall; her body rose up.

John Motton studied his Appointments Book. He had had no appointments today or tomorrow; he had only two appointments next week. He would finish his paper discrediting Fowler; he needed to stop all those mechanics flocking to the Institute night after night, stupid as sheep. He took his father's pipe out of the draw and tapped the tobacco out on to the desk. His father's desk, his father's books, the porcelain head, the globe, the birds in the cabinet, his father's measuring tape. His father's measuring: pulling the tape round, tight, rough—angry—the callipers cold on his temples, the measurements, at different times of day and evening; after exercise, before and after food; comparing the earlier and the later measurements; the accusations. The oak-panelled Room, the closed shutters, the open shutters, being studied with the magnifying glass under the window, now under the lamp, the father's eye appearing huge on the other side of the glass. And John, sitting absolutely still as he had been taught, controlling the muscles in his face, watching the eye appearing and receding. Sometimes the father would sigh. Then he would carefully and slowly put away his measuring instruments, his callipers and his notebooks, and lay his head down on the desk. After several minutes, perhaps ten minutes, during which time the boy was required to keep absolutely still, the father would rise up a little and grip the bridge of his own nose with his thumb and forefinger, and the son hadn't yet been given permission to leave, so the young

171

Motton would remain, rigid within the cage of his chest until his father spoke.

'Either you, my own son, have criminal, even sexually perverse proclivities,' he would say, 'or Phrenology itself is wrong.'

Neither proposition could be countenanced.

And all the time, throughout all this, Mother would be rustling and flapping in and out of the Room on spurious errands, delivering a letter, bringing a fresh pot of tea, burbling like a pigeon.

John Motton put down his pipe, and began to take his phrenology books out of the bookcase. He stacked them on his desk. He pulled out the journals with their yellow covers. He stared at one of them for a while, and slowly split it along its sewn spine.

Mrs. Peake whispers, 'They have come together to pray for you, my dear—your ladies, dear, they have brought flowers and fruits, and a pair of kid gloves.'

All of Alice's ladies together: each wearing one of her hats. They are in the room. How beautiful they look.

Miss Thirsk stands tall with her willow neck, her dark shining hair, the little smirk at the mouth. She is wearing the bashlik hood—merino wool, cream, with velvet and satin trims. The light shines from her skin, she swishes her cream cloak, her leather boots are the colour of duck eggs. *'She brings gentlemen to me by her magic, and she knows my thoughts.'*

Mrs. Zaphinov, a crush, a jangle, a circus of froth and fold—enormous above Alice, lush with chiffon and silk and muslin, coiled and swathed, a great mound at her head. She swaddles Alice in her gowns. *'I must have you, Miss Alice Heapy, for you have the measure of me!'*

And Miss Alicia Linden, aswoop with colour and raiment, the pairs in the ark all over patterned—she is the one talking now. '*Miss Alice Heapy, trace your finger over these: the orange-blossom, the ant-hill, the palm-leaf. You made them from exquisite cloth, from the cloth of your soul, my dear. That is why they sparkle, why they live. My sister used to call me drab, a box, a panel in an oak-lined room: and now I am an ark, a menagerie, an aviary. Take this jewel, it is crystal, it is formed by the sweat of bees. Tell me, Alice, how you knew?*'

She, Miss Alicia Linden, stands up straight and swings her arms in the air; she makes the shape of the globe with her arms. Her layers of turquoise satin spin in the half-light. She sings: ra-la-ra-la. '*It is not because of him but because of you, my dear. He only gave me a word. A little word.*' She whispers it now: *Wonder*, her lips making a triangle in her long face. She presses her gloved hand over the organ of *Wonder* at the front of her head and strokes it round.

And now Mrs. Belinda Motton: a bird, a mouse, a pencil. She laughs her stair-winding laugh. She is tiny amongst Mrs. Zaphinov and Miss Linden. She cries into Alice's hand, which lies palm up away from the bed. Alice feels the salt warmth, wet and dry at once, on her palm, running through her fingers, tickling, trickling—try to hold on. Alice tries to hold on to each of Belinda Motton's warm tears. She did not peck Alice when she was least expecting it. She did not fly up to the eaves; and now she is mourning *her*, Alice Heapy—who lifted her from dull olive to cranberry silk. '*Here: my favourite hat,*' she says, '*it whispers to me when I place it on my head: my hair listens, my scalp tingles, I am ears.*' She unwraps the cranberry hat, she unwraps it slowly, running her fingers round the brim, up into the inside of the crown, she places it on her head, moving it slightly, forward, back, a little to the left, back to the right, as all ladies do when they place their hats on their heads. *Sssh. Sssh, let us both listen, my dear, let us listen.*

Mrs. Zaphinov and Miss Linden are breathing, doors are banging, and then they hear it, the singing, high, higher, beyond all reach, like honey, in the silk of darkness.

Next, next, next. It is Isabella Raleigh. She steps forward where she has remained closed and silent behind the others. She is detached, she is neutral. She is grand, military—she is precise. She bends towards Alice, her face porcelain. She kisses Alice's forehead as if Alice is her child. Isabella Raleigh is here, cool porcelain, with the tartan square secured with pins. She loves him, Isabella loves John Motton—a love that doesn't attach itself strongly to its object, yet it is love. When she once again stands upright, Isabella Raleigh snaps her fingers; the authoritative sound of her middle finger snaps down on the pad-base of her thumb. She does it again, to beckon the silence towards her—to make a mark within the silence. Isabella marks Alice with her finger-snap. And then Miss Linden is taking fresh flowers out of her hat and placing them in a waterglass. Mrs. Peake is rapping at the door again, she is appearing and disappearing.

'Dearest sweet sister, come back to us. Take the cold water from your jug, take these violets, Alice. Come back to us, Alice.'

They are saying, come back, a little each day. With each movement of the light, come a little way in again, slowly, without exertion. Who is saying this? It is Alicia Linden. She came back in, she moved from oak panel to radiance. She is saying to Alice, quietly now, above her body, 'Try to come back, Alice, just a little at a time.' The voice is the fine clear call of a tropical bird, clear and pure, fresh as bright green leaves in rain. A tropical bird is calling her: how shall she answer?

Acknowledgements

I am very grateful to the following people for their close and insightful readings of early and late drafts: Chris Drury, Steve Holland, Mary Hooper, Kate Honeyford, Jackie Kay, Judith Keyston, Ariane Koek, Trish MacCourt, Jane McLoughlin, and Jane Wildgoose. I would also like to thank Sheelagh Killeen, Lil Scott at Cosprop and the Booth Museum in Brighton. Special thanks, too, to Jan and Mike Fortune-Wood at Cinnamon Press.